THE WORLD'S CLASSICS

HARRY HEATHCOTE OF GANGOIL

ANTHONY TROLLOPE (1815–82), the son of a failing London barrister, was brought up an awkward and unhappy youth amidst debt and privation. His mother maintained the family by writing, but Anthony's own first novel did not appear until 1847, when he had at length established a successful Civil Service career in the Post Office, from which he retired in 1867. After a slow start, he achieved fame, with 47 novels and some 16 other books, and sales sometimes topping 100,000. He was acclaimed an unsurpassed portraitist of the lives of the professional and landed classes, especially in his perennially popular *Chronicles of Barsetshire* (1855–67), and his six brilliant Palliser novels (1864–80). His fascinating *Autobiography* (1883) recounts his successes with an enthusiasm which stems from memories of a miserable youth. Throughout the 1870s he developed new styles of fiction, but was losing critical favour by the time of his death.

P. D. EDWARDS is Professor of English at the University of Queensland. His books include *Anthony Trollope's Son in Australia: The Life and Letters of F. J. A. Trollope* (1982), and he has edited Trollope's *Autobiography*, *Framley Parsonage*, and *Rachel Ray* for World's Classics.

THE WORLD'S CLASSICS

ANTHONY TROLLOPE

Harry Heathcote
of Gangoil

A Tale of Australian Bushlife

Edited with an Introduction by
P. D. EDWARDS

Oxford   New York
OXFORD UNIVERSITY PRESS
1992

Oxford University Press, Walton Street, Oxford OX2 6DP

Oxford New York Toronto
Delhi Bombay Calcutta Madras Karachi
Petaling Jaya Singapore Hong Kong Tokyo
Nairobi Dar es Salaam Cape Town
Melbourne Auckland

and associated companies in
Berlin Ibadan

Oxford is a trade mark of Oxford University Press

British Library Cataloguing in Publication Data
Data available

Library of Congress Cataloging in Publication Data

Trollope, Anthony, 1815–1882.
Harry Heathcote of Gangoil: a tale of Australian bush life /
Anthony Trollope: edited with an introduction by P.D. Edwards.
p. cm.—(The World's classics)
Includes bibliographical references.
I. Edwards, Peter David. II. Title. III. Series.
PR5684.H3 1992 823'.8—dc20 91–42963
ISBN 0-19-282846-0

Typeset by Pure Tech Corporation (India)
Printed in Great Britain by
BPCC Hazells Ltd.
Aylesbury, Bucks

CONTENTS

CONTENTS

INTRODUCTION

THOUGH one of the shortest and most unpretentious of Anthony Trollope's forty-seven novels, *Harry Heathcote of Gangoil* is distinctive in at least three regards. It is Trollope's longest Christmas story, and the only one published on its own as a book—at any rate in England and during his lifetime.[1] It is his only novel set entirely in the New World, unless *The Fixed Period*, set in an imaginary country in the South Pacific, is also included in this category. And Harry Heathcote is his only hero or major character avowedly, and more or less consistently, modelled on a living person. As some of the original reviewers commented, the novel provided a further refreshing example of its author's readiness to strike out in new directions, diverging from the familiar paths that were most congenial to him and to his readership.

During the 1870s the demand for new novels by Trollope began to slacken, and this no doubt helps to account for his increasing willingness to turn his hand to Christmas stories in spite of the contempt for them which he proclaimed, with characteristic forthrightness, in his *Autobiography*, written in 1876:

I feel, with regard to literature, somewhat as I suppose an upholsterer and undertaker feels when he is called upon to supply a funeral. He has to supply it, however distasteful it may be. It is his business, and he will starve if he neglect it. So have I felt that, when anything in the shape of a novel was required, I was bound to produce it. Nothing can be more distasteful to me than

[1] Another Christmas story 'Christmas Day at Thompson Hall', only a fraction the length of *Harry Heathcote*, was published as a monograph in the United States in 1876, and Trollope's last Christmas story, 'The Two Heroines of Plumplington', was published as a book in England in 1948, 65 years after his death. It too was much shorter than *Harry Heathcote*.

to have to give a relish of Christmas to what I write. I feel the humbug implied by the nature of the order. A Christmas story, in the proper sense, should be the ebullition of some mind anxious to instil others with a desire for Christmas religious thought, or Christmas festivities,—or, better still, with Christmas charity. Such was the case with Dickens when he wrote his two first Christmas stories. But since that the things written annually—all of which have been fixed to Christmas like children's toys to a Christmas tree—have had no real savour of Christmas about them. I had done two or three before [*Harry Heathcote of Gangoil*]. Alas! at this very moment I have one to write, which I have promised to supply within three weeks of this time . . . as to which I have in vain been cudgelling my brain for the last month.[2]

The 'two or three' Christmas stories Trollope had written before *Harry Heathcote of Gangoil* were followed by six more between 1873 and his death in 1882—including the one over which he was cudgelling his brains in 1876, 'Christmas at Thompson Hall'.[3] It was in a Christmas story, 'The Two Heroines of Plumplington', written in the final year of his life, that he made a belated return to the 'dear county' of Barsetshire, more than fifteen years after he had left it for good and only a year or so after he had assured a correspondent that he never would return to it.[4] Without the disarming humbug of the Christmas story, the spirit of hanging children's toys on a Christmas tree, this was an indulgence that one imagines he would have gone on denying himself till the end. Similarly, it seems unlikely that he would have ventured on a tale recognizably about his younger son and his problems, but for a comfortable feeling that his usual standards of realism could safely be relaxed

[2] *An Autobiography* (World's Classics edn., Oxford, 1980), 356–7.
[3] All of Trollope's Christmas stories except *Harry Heathcote* are collected in the Trollope Society edn. of the complete short stories of Trollope, vol. i. *The Christmas Stories* (1990).
[4] Letter to Henry Howard, in *The Letters of Anthony Trollope*, ed. N. John Hall (Stanford, Calif., 1983), ii. 920.

in a Christmas story, especially one set at the opposite end of the planet.

What the framework of the Christmas story offered him was above all the opportunity for some wishful thinking on his son's behalf. The essential requirement of the species, as established by Dickens in the 1840s, was a spectacular resolution of class-conflicts and a patching up of personal differences, preferably consummated over Christmas dinner at the end of the tale. Christmas, which ushered in the restoration of hope for all mankind, had to be shown doing the same for beleaguered individuals, ensuring their worldly if not eternal salvation and answering their most fervent prayers. In Trollope's novel this is effected by the formation of an alliance between the young hero and the representative of the class which poses the greatest threat to his livelihood and perhaps even his personal safety. As an additional Christmas present the alliance brings the hero's sister-in-law an offer of marriage from the only eligible man in the district.

Of all the exotic regions that Trollope painstakingly toured and wrote about—the West Indies, North America, Australia and New Zealand, Ceylon, South Africa, Iceland—Australia was the one in which he spent most time and had most reason to feel a close and continuing interest. His first visit lasted a full year, from 27 July 1871 to 29 July 1872, and included extensive travelling in all six colonies as well as quite lengthy stays at his son's sheep station, Mortray, about 250 miles west of Sydney. (Even his second visit, a rushed business trip without his wife, lasted nearly four months.) In addition to *Harry Heathcote of Gangoil* his travels around the colonies in 1871–2 produced the evocative and convincingly realistic gold-mining scenes in a later novel, *John Caldigate* (1879) and the almost encyclopaedic travel book, *Australia and New Zealand*, published in two volumes early in 1873. The latter, in particular, establishes beyond doubt Trollope's credentials for writing realistically about the social, economic, and climatic problems afflicting his Australian son. It expatiates knowledgeably and at great length on the social conflict which provides the mainspring of the plot of *Harry Heathcote of Gangoil*: the bitter contest between squatters like his son, who ran their flocks mainly on Crown land, and the free-selectors who were being encouraged by generous land laws to buy up the squatters' choicest pastures. But the harsh realities of the situation as he had presented them in his travel book are significantly softened in his Christmas story with his son as thinly disguised hero. In effect he allowed himself to simulate a degree of ignorance, to forget a little of what he knew, or even to retreat deliberately into realms that he did not know at all.

Perhaps the most striking example was his decision to locate his story on the banks of the Mary River in southern Queensland. His manuscript shows that this was only his third choice. Previously he had considered first the Condamine River, which flows through the Darling Downs, also in southern Queensland, and then the Lachlan River, quite close to his son's property in central western New South Wales. These were both areas that he certainly knew better than the lower Mary River valley, much of which he hardly saw at all when he visited it in 1871, having travelled through it after dark and stayed overnight in the small town of Tiaro, apparently without visiting any farms.[5] But it was no doubt the very fact that he was relatively ignorant of the locality that dictated his choice of it in preference to the other two. Given the strong possibility that his son would be recognized as the model for Harry Heathcote, there was an obvious danger that some of Harry's black-guardly enemies might be mistaken for neighbours of his son's, whom the author could be accused of traducing under

[5] See *Anthony Trollope: Australia*, ed. P. D. Edwards and R. B. Joyce (St. Lucia, Queensland, 1967), 117. This is a reprint of the Australian section of Trollope's *Australia and New Zealand*.

the cloak of fiction, settling scores on his son's behalf. The safest setting from this point of view was clearly a district in which he knew no squatters, free-selectors, or disgruntled farm labourers at all.

Trollope probably felt that for a Christmas story commissioned by an English magazine (the *Graphic*) one part of Australia would do as well as another, so long as the plot and circumstances seemed broadly authentic and the culmination was a bush Christmas. And in truth no reader's enjoyment of the novel or belief in its basic realism is likely to be unduly disturbed either by the geographical and historical errors resulting from Trollope's choice of location, or by the more conscious liberties he took for his son's sake and the Christmas reader's. By Christmas 1871, when the events related in the novel take place, the lower Mary Valley was predominantly a sugar-growing area, and Harry Heathcote would certainly have lost more than one small segment of his riverfront land to free-selectors; moreover the land near the river had never really been hospitable to sheep, being too wet, subject not so much to the bushfires that threaten to immolate Gangoil nearly every summer as to repeated summer floods—one of which had in fact occurred earlier in 1871.

These are errors that Trollope might have blushed about, if anyone had been brave enough to point them out to him, and he would also have been disappointed by sarcastic comments on his imitations, mercifully intermittent, of the peculiarities of Australian speech. He would not have been abashed, however, if taken to task for his more deliberate departures from strict probability: his decision to let Harry off not only with a lone free-selector, hardly making a dint in his choicest land, but also with one who is his equal in education, intelligence, fortune, and almost—but reassuringly not quite—in birth (p. 27). Since such a man obviously would not dream of stealing the young squatter's sheep or setting fire to his grass, as free-selectors commonly did or were accused of doing, the immediate threat to the hero's survival has to be shown as coming from a different quarter, and a very convenient one from Trollope's point of view: namely a fellow squatter and his family. The fact that, though nominally a member of his own class, the fellow squatter happens to be a rascally ex-convict with no education or social graces is largely beside the point; the important thing is that he enables Trollope to avoid casting the free-selector, the representative of the class whose cause he had publicly espoused in *Australia and New Zealand*, in the role of villain, while simultaneously giving the lonely squatter an ally and companion more or less of his own rank. And Harry needs such a companion to check the feudal 'imperiousness' which aggravates the threats he faces, by needlessly adding disaffected former employees to the ranks of his enemies—though Trollope had made it clear in *Australia and New Zealand* that to some extent such men were always among the natural class enemies of the squatters, regardless of the treatment they received from them as masters.

As one would expect, critics back in England were more than content to take on trust the authenticity and typicality of the novel's pictures of Australian life. Richard Holt Hutton, Trollope's favourite reviewer, who had never been to Australia himself, boldly proclaimed that it threw more light on colonial life than any number of blue books and had no doubt that its 'effective and interesting picture of the conditions of rural life in Queensland', which Trollope must have seen with his own eyes, would 'ensure good sales in Queensland and the other colonies'.[6] But Hutton clearly had no conception at all of the touchiness of colonial sensitivities when condescension on the part of the mother country was suspected, as it nearly always was—particularly by radicals bent on eliminating all vestiges of the English

---

[6] *Spectator*, 48 (20 Feb. 1875), 247–8.

class system from the new land. Even *Australia and New Zealand* had aroused considerable resentment, despite Trollope's unreserved support for the free-selectors against the squatters and his enthusiastic praise of the Australian working man, whom he found generally more self-respecting, better behaved, and vastly better off than his opposite number in England. One review which warmly praised it for its 'truthfulness' was nevertheless headed, with seemingly gratuitous rudeness, 'Mr Trollope's Latest Work of Fiction', and another, while not denying its acuteness of observation and its 'unbiased admiration' for the colonies, nevertheless took it for granted that Trollope felt superior to the colonists and accused him, though without citing any examples, of writing 'with the air of a man who believes that he is conferring a favour upon [them] by making them the groundwork of a book'.[7] The prickly defensiveness displayed here—a by-product of the attitude known in Australia nowadays as the 'cultural cringe'—would have made it a matter of principle for Australian reviewers to avoid responding to *Harry Heathcote of Gangoil* with the grateful enthusiasm that R. H. Hutton expected, even if they had been no more aware than he of its errors of fact and unpalatable political implications.

Although commissioned by an English magazine, *Harry Heathcote of Gangoil* was in fact published first in Australia, being serialized in the Melbourne *Age* from 15 November 1873 to 3 January 1874. (The Christmas number of the *Graphic*, in which it first appeared in England, was not issued until Christmas Day, 1873.) As it happened, *Australia and New Zealand*, which had been published as a book in February 1873, was still being serialized in another Melbourne paper, the *Australasian*, when *Harry Heathcote of Gangoil* began appearing in the *Age*. Australian commentators were thus

---

[7] Brisbane *Courier* (14 Mar. 1873), 2; Melbourne *Argus* (21 June 1873), Supplement, 1.

able to pass judgement on the novel in advance of their English confrères, and were also given a second opportunity—and in many ways a better one—to voice their resentment at Trollope's supposed condescension and factual and political errors in *Australia and New Zealand* while that work, too, was still coming out. One of those who gleefully seized the opportunity was a leader-writer in the Melbourne *Herald* who angrily demanded to know why an Australian newspaper that could have employed the talents of reputable colonial novelists who knew Australia well—including Marcus Clarke, the author of *For the Term of His Natural Life*—had instead preferred to 'pay an unfortunate adle-headed old gentleman who, as *Punch* very wittily put it, drove through the colonies on an express locomotive, to libel us at home, and make us the laughing-stock of our own people'.[8] As an example of the 'drivel' and 'utter rot' that Trollope perpetrated in the novel, he cited the sequence in which Harry Heathcote is described as 'continually riding about all night and discovering nothing' and then as galloping through the bush to see who is felling trees after he has heard the sound of an axe in the middle of the night. The *Punch* to which the writer in the *Herald* referred was not the London but the Melbourne *Punch*, and its wit had been exhibited in a two-part parody of Trollope's novel, entitled '*Harry Hartshorn, of Tinfoil*, by Anthony Dollup'.[9] In this Mr Dollup at one point describes the hero as encountering a 'cangeroo' with a tail 'longer than any I may have written'; the rather dubious geography of Trollope's novel is satirized by the location of Tinfoil in the centre of the wild Victorian bush on the Swan River in

[8] *Herald* (9 Dec. 1873).
[9] *Melbourne Punch* (20 Nov. 1873), 167, and (4 Dec. 1873), 177. Another Trollope novel serialized in a Melbourne paper in 1873 was *The Eustace Diamonds*, and *Punch*'s parody of *Harry Heathcote* concludes with an announcement by 'Cangeroo' that he has found the Eustace diamonds out in the bush.

Queensland; and Trollope's self-conscious and not always accurate display of his familiarity with the oddities of Australian speech is mercilessly mimicked. (Examples of the kind of geographical and linguistic slips that aroused the parodist's mirth are recorded in the notes to the present edition.) Hot on the heels of *Punch's* parody followed a topical couplet in Garnet Walch's Christmas pantomime, *Australia Felix; or Harlequin, Laughing Jackass and the Magic Bat,* which opened in Melbourne on Boxing Day 1873:

> May Trollope make you, oh! how low to grovel,
> The hero of his next *Australian* novel —[10]

again conveying, implicitly at least, the impression that Trollope expected the colonials to cringe for his favour and that some of them would always be mean spirited enough to oblige.

Trollope's decision to model his hero on his younger son ('The Harry Heathcote is my boy Frederic,—or very much the same,' he told a friend)[11] effectively forced him to relax his usual standards of moral and psychological as well as of social realism. It did not prevent him from making good use of the knowledge and understanding of the etiquette and style of the station homestead and the nature of the work and work-places of the station itself which he had acquired during his visits to Frederic's property, Mortray; and it gave him a useful opportunity to deliver a gentle warning to Fred about the unnecessary hostility his imperiousness might arouse. But he clearly could not contemplate delving into his son's character and perhaps exposing deeper flaws, more serious grounds for moral concern, as he would have with an imaginary hero. Not only had the

[10] *Australia Felix; or Harlequin, Laughing Jackass and the Magic Bat,* ed. Veronica Kelly (St Lucia, Queensland, 1988), II. iii. 63–4.
[11] Letter to Mary Holmes, 15 June 1876, in *The Letters of Anthony Trollope,* ii. 693.

xvi   *Introduction*

hero's problems in a harsh, even dangerous environment
to be presented as amenable to relatively easy and palatable
solutions, requiring little more than changes of attitude on
his part or new personal alignments, but he himself had to
be viewed, by the author and by his own family and friends,
with an unusually benign and myopic gaze. (This is not to
suggest, however, that Trollope had or felt that he had any
grounds for serious anxiety about his son's character as
distinct from his social and economic situation.) As indi-
cated in the notes to the present edition, Harry Heathcote's
situation mirrors that of Fred Trollope in most important
respects (apart from the location of his sheep station), but
there is one striking and revealing difference: Harry's station is four times as large as Fred's and carries three times
as many sheep. If Fred and his father had had the capital
to afford a station the size of Harry's, the fate which
overtook him only two years after the novel was written,
and which his father must have seen as always on the cards,
might well have been averted. When Anthony returned to
Australia in 1875 he and Fred decided that Mortray would
have to be sold, at a loss of over £4,600. But Anthony was
at pains to assure his elder son that Fred was in no way
to blame for the misfortune.[12]

The broader political perspective in which Anthony saw
his son's situation and the conflict between squatters and
free-selectors generally is beautifully delineated in a passage
in his *Australia and New Zealand*:

There is something admirable, or at least enviable, in the rock-fast
conviction of men, the leading principles of whose lives have been
formed by the combined strength of education, custom, and
interest. It is so with the Australian squatter, who does not feel
more sure that he himself will be injured by the operation of the
free-selector than that the free-selector himself will be ruined by
it. The squatter produces wool, and knows that wool is the staple

[12] Ibid. ii. 679.

produce of the colonies. To his thinking, success in wool means Australian greatness, and any drawback on that success, Australian misfortune. Any laws which may interfere with his pastoral and almost patriarchal views of life seem to him to emanate from democracy and the devil. He gets into parliament himself . . . at great personal inconvenience, feeling but little personal ambition as to his seat,—only that he may check the making of such laws. He knows that there must and will be land-laws in his colony, having the same melancholy certainty in the success of democracy and the devil as that which pervades the mind of an English Tory. He will even frame the land-law himself,—the very land-law which is to give power to the free-selector,—as the Tory in England has framed laws for extended suffrage and the like. The English Tory when he is among his friends does not scruple to declare his hatred for the work of his own hands. In parliament it is necessary to be conciliatory, ready to yield, and almost submissive;—but in private life every one knows of course that these changes are the work of democracy and the devil. It is really the same with the Australian Tory, as with his cousin at home. There must be land-laws, and the law must throw open the squatter's run to the rapacity of the free-selector;—but not the less is the free-selector an abomination and a curse. Personally, I love a squatter. I like to hear his grievances and to sympathize with them. I can make myself at home with him;—and can talk to him of his sheep more comfortably than I can to a miner of his gold, or a merchant of his dealings. But on principle I take the part of the free-selector.[13]

The conflict which Trollope owns to here between his heart and his head, his sympathies and his principles, his instinctive Toryism and his rational liberalism, informs all his writing and is the secret of the broad pragmatic tolerance and understanding that make it so appealing to twentieth-century readers. In one of her stories George Eliot describes herself as letting her imagination 'do a little Toryism by the sly'[14] and Trollope often indulges his in similar fashion.

---

[13] *Anthony Trollope: Australia*, 200-1.
[14] 'The Sad Fortunes of the Rev. Amos Barton', in *Scenes of Clerical Life* (Clarendon edn., Oxford, 1985), 7.

Seldom, however, as prodigally as in *Harry Heathcote of Gangoil*. For here his Toryism is engaged on behalf of his own son, from whom he had parted, perhaps for ever, two years previously, gasping out his pain in his diary: 'Bad farewell to my dearest Boy—very sad—Ah me!'[15] At one point in *Harry Heathcote of Gangoil* the hero is pictured, or pictures himself, as an Abraham who has departed from his father's house to make for himself and his seed a great nation in a strange land (p. 92). And this fanciful vision of his son as Old Testament patriarch, triumphing at Christmas-time over his human and natural enemies, was all that Trollope was to have to comfort him in the years that followed, as Fred lost Mortray and was then unable, because of illness, to work another property that he had bought, further out in the wilderness. In a different, more modest way Fred was destined to make good his father's prophecy nevertheless, achieving respect and reasonable prosperity as a long-serving official of the Lands Department in New South Wales and leaving behind, in Sydney and other parts of Australia, a number of descendants—the only surviving descendants of Anthony Trollope—among them the inheritors of the family baronetcy from which Anthony himself had been several times removed. But sadly Anthony did not see his son again after his second visit to Australia in 1875 and Fred did not see his mother and his native country again until 1903, by which time he was almost an old man.[16]

[15] Cited in R. H. Super, *The Chronicler of Barsetshire: A Life of Anthony Trollope* (Ann Arbor, Mich., 1988), 304.

[16] See P. D. Edwards, *Anthony Trollope's Son in Australia: The Life and Letters of F. J. A. Trollope* (St Lucia, Queensland, 1982).

NOTE ON THE TEXT

THE text of the present edition is based on that of the first
edition published by Sampson Low in October 1874. This
edition sold at the standard price of half a guinea (10*s.* 6*d.*)
but was followed almost immediately by a cheaper illustrated edition, also published by Sampson Low, which sold
at 5*s.*

Previously the novel had been serialized in the Melbourne
Age, 15 November 1873–3 January 1874, before appearing
as the Christmas number of the *Graphic*, dated 25 December
1873. The unusually long interval between its appearance
in the *Graphic* and its publication as a book probably
accounts in part for the speed with which the cheaper
illustrated edition followed the first edition. An American
edition, published by Harper and Brothers, had appeared
before the first English one.

The text of the serialization in the *Age* was evidently set
from sheets supplied by the *Graphic*, but a few minor
corrections were made. There are few significant variations
between the *Graphic* text and that of the first edition.

A comparison between the author's manuscript, which is
in the Beinecke Library, Yale University, and the first
edition reveals the following apparent misreadings of the
manuscript which have been corrected in the present edition:

p. 4, line 28	*seldom* but seldom MS
p. 19, line 32	*ill-constituted* ill-conditioned MS
p. 29, line 19	*and tall like Heathcote* not tall like Heathcote MS
p. 39, line 15	*suspense* suspicion MS
p. 59, lines 22 and 26	*Darnley Downs* Darling Downs MS

p. 61, line 28	*scruf* scruff MS
p. 62, line 35	*a large portion* a large practice MS
p. 71, line 19	*clenched* clinched MS
p. 81, line 2	*damage* danger MS

One or two minor errors which obviously escaped Trollope's attention both in his manuscript and in the first edition have now been corrected, in most cases silently.

SELECT BIBLIOGRAPHY

INVALUABLE aids to the reader of any of Trollope's novels include his autobiography, *An Autobiography* (written, 1876; first published, 1883; World's Classics edition, Oxford, ed. P. D. Edwards, 1980); his letters, *The Letters of Anthony Trollope*, ed. N. John Hall (Stanford, Calif., 1983); Michael Sadleir, *Trollope: A Bibliography* (London, 1928); R. H. Super, *The Chronicler of Barsetshire: A Life of Anthony Trollope* (Ann. Arbor, Mich., 1988) and N. John Hall, *Trollope: A Biography* (Oxford, 1991); and Donald Smalley (ed.), *Anthony Trollope: The Critical Heritage* (London, 1969).

There are useful discussions of *Harry Heathcote of Gangoil* in R. H. Super's and N. John Hall's books listed above and in Robert Tracy, *Trollope's Later Novels* (Berkeley, Calif., 1978). The best guide to the social and historical background to the novel is Trollope's travel book, *Australia and New Zealand* (1873); a scholarly edition of the part of this book dealing with Australia, edited by P. D. Edwards and R. B. Joyce, was published by the University of Queensland Press in 1967, under the title *Anthony Trollope: Australia*. It includes an appendix (Appendix 3) on Trollope's 'Australian' novels, *Harry Heathcote of Gangoil* and *John Caldigate*. An account of the Australian career of Trollope's younger son, who was the model for Harry Heathcote, is given in P. D. Edwards, *Anthony Trollope's Son in Australia: the Life and Letters of F. J. A. Trollope (1847–1910)* (St Lucia, Queensland, 1982).

A CHRONOLOGY OF
ANTHONY TROLLOPE

VIRTUALLY all Trollope's fiction after *Framley Parsonage* (1860–1) appeared first in serial form, with book publication usually coming just prior to the final instalment of the serial.

1815   (24 Apr.) Born at 16 Keppel Street, Bloomsbury, the fourth son of Thomas and Frances Trollope.
        (Summer?) Family moves to Harrow-on-the-Hill.

1823   To Harrow School as a day-boy.

1825   To a private school at Sunbury.

1827   To school at Winchester College.

1830   Removed from Winchester and returned to Harrow.

1834   (Apr.) The family flees to Bruges to escape creditors.
        (Nov.) Accepts a junior clerkship in the General Post Office, London.

1841   (Sept.) Made Postal Surveyor's Clerk at Banagher, King's County, Ireland.

1843   (mid-Sept.) Begins work on his first novel, *The Macdermots of Ballycloran*.

1844   (11 June) Marries Rose Heseltine.
        (Aug.) Transferred to Clonmel, County Tipperary.

1846   (13 Mar.) Son, Henry Merivale Trollope, born.

1847   *The Macdermots of Ballycloran*, published in 3 vols. (Newby).
        (27 Sept.) Son, Frederic James Anthony Trollope, born.

1848   *The Kellys and the O'Kellys; or Landlords and Tenants*, 3 vols. (Colburn).
        (Autumn) Moves to Mallow, County Cork.

1850   *La Vendée; An Historical Romance*, 3 vols. (Colburn).
        Writes *The Noble Jilt* (a play, published 1923).

1851   (1 Aug.) Sent to south-west of England on special postal mission.

1853   (29 July) Begins *The Warden* (the first of the Barsetshire novels).
       (29 Aug.) Moves to Belfast as Acting Surveyor.

1854   (9 Oct.) Appointed Surveyor of Northern District of Ireland.

1855   *The Warden*, 1 vol. (Longman).
       Writes *The New Zealander*.
       (June) Moves to Donnybrook, Dublin.

1857   *Barchester Towers*, 3 vols. (Longman).

1858   *The Three Clerks*, 3 vols. (Bentley).
       Doctor Thorne, 3 vols. (Chapman & Hall).
       (Jan.) Departs for Egypt on Post Office business.
       (Mar.) Visits Holy Land.
       (Apr.–May) Returns via Malta, Gibraltar, and Spain.
       (May–Sept.) Visits Scotland and north of England on postal business.
       (16 Nov.) Leaves for the West Indies on postal mission.

1859   *The Bertrams*, 3 vols. (Chapman & Hall).
       The West Indies and the Spanish Main, 1 vol. (Chapman & Hall).
       (3 July) Arrives home.
       (Nov.) Leaves Ireland; settles at Waltham Cross, Hertfordshire, after being appointed Surveyor of the Euston District of England.

1860   *Castle Richmond*, 3 vols. (Chapman & Hall).
       First serialized fiction, *Framley Parsonage*, published in the *Cornhill Magazine*.
       (Oct.) Visits, with his wife, his mother, and brother in Florence; makes the acquaintance of Kate Field, a 22-year-old American for whom he forms a romantic attachment.

1861   *Framley Parsonage*, 3 vols. (Smith, Elder).
       Tales of All Countries, 1 vol. (Chapman & Hall).
       (24 Aug.) Leaves for America to write a travel book.

1862   *Orley Farm*, 2 vols. (Chapman & Hall).
       North America, 2 vols. (Chapman & Hall).
       The Struggles of Brown, Jones and Robinson: By One of the

Firm, 1 vol. (New York, Harper—an American piracy; first English edition, 1870, Smith, Elder).
(25 Mar.) Arrives home from America.
(5 Apr.) Elected to the Garrick Club.

1863   *Tales of All Countries*, Second Series, 1 vol. (Chapman & Hall).
Rachel Ray, 2 vols. (Chapman & Hall).
(6 Oct.) Death of his mother, Mrs Frances Trollope.

1864   *The Small House at Allington*, 2 vols. (Smith, Elder).
(12 Apr.) Elected a member of the Athenaeum Club.

1865   *Can You Forgive Her?*, 2 vols. (Chapman & Hall).
Miss Mackenzie, 1 vol. (Chapman & Hall).
Hunting Sketches, 1 vol. (Chapman & Hall).

1866   *The Belton Estate*, 3 vols. (Chapman & Hall).
Travelling Sketches, 1 vol. (Chapman & Hall).
Clergymen of the Church of England, 1 vol. (Chapman & Hall).

1867   *Nina Balatka*, 2 vols. (Blackwood).
The Claverings, 2 vols. (Smith, Elder).
The Last Chronicle of Barset, 2 vols. (Smith, Elder).
Lotta Schmidt and Other Stories, 1 vol. (Strahan).
(1 Sept.) Resigns from the Post Office.
Assumes editorship of *Saint Pauls Magazine*.

1868   *Linda Tressel*, 2 vols. (Blackwood).
(11 Apr.) Leaves London for the United States on postal mission.
(26 July) Returns from America.
(Nov.) Stands unsuccessfully as Liberal candidate for Beverley, Yorkshire.

1869   *Phineas Finn; the Irish Member*, 2 vols. (Virtue & Co).
He Knew He Was Right, 2 vols. (Strahan).
Did He Steal It? A Comedy in Three Acts (a version of *The Last Chronicle of Barset*, privately printed by Virtue & Co).

1870   *The Vicar of Bullhampton*, 1 vol. (Bradbury, Evans).
An Editor's Tales, 1 vol. (Strahan).
The Commentaries of Caesar, 1 vol. (Blackwood).
(Jan.–July) Eased out of *Saint Pauls Magazine*.

1871   *Sir Harry Hotspur of Humblethwaite*, 1 vol. (Hurst & Blackett).
        Ralph the Heir, 3 vols. (Hurst & Blackett).
        (Apr.) Gives up house at Waltham Cross.
        (24 May) Sails to Australia to visit his son.
        (27 July) Arrives at Melbourne.

1872   *The Golden Lion of Granpere*, 1 vol. (Tinsley).
        (Jan.–Oct.) Travelling in Australia and New Zealand.
        (Dec.) Returns via the United States.

1873   *The Eustace Diamonds*, 3 vols. (Chapman & Hall).
        Australia and New Zealand, 2 vols. (Chapman & Hall).
        (Apr.) Settles in Montagu Square, London.

1874   *Phineas Redux*, 2 vols. (Chapman & Hall).
        Lady Anna, 2 vols. (Chapman & Hall).
        Harry Heathcote of Gangoil. A Tale of Australian Bush Life, 1
        vol. (Sampson Low).

1875   *The Way We Live Now*, 2 vols. (Chapman & Hall).
        (1 Mar.) Leaves for Australia via Brindisi, the Suez
        Canal, and Ceylon.
        (4 May) Arrives in Australia.
        (Aug.–Oct.) Sailing homewards.
        (Oct.) Begins *An Autobiography*.

1876   *The Prime Minister*, 4 vols. (Chapman & Hall).

1877   *The American Senator*, 3 vols. (Chapman & Hall).
        (29 June) Leaves for South Africa.
        (11 Dec.) Sails for home.

1878   *South Africa*, 2 vols. (Chapman & Hall).
        Is He Popenjoy?, 3 vols. (Chapman & Hall).
        (June–July) Travels to Iceland in the yacht *Mastiff. How
        the 'Mastiffs' Went to Iceland*, 1 vol. (privately printed,
        Virtue & Co).

1879   *An Eye for an Eye*, 2 vols. (Chapman & Hall).
        Thackeray, 1 vol. (Macmillan).
        John Candigate, 3 vols. (Chapman & Hall).
        Cousin Henry, 2 vols. (Chapman & Hall).

1880   *The Duke's Children*, 3 vols. (Chapman & Hall).

       The Life of Cicero, 2 vols. (Chapman & Hall).
       (July) Settles at South Harting, Sussex, near Petersfield.

1881   *Dr Wortle's School*, 2 vols. (Chapman & Hall).
       Ayala's Angel, 3 vols. (Chapman & Hall).

1882   *Why Frau Frohmann Raised Her Prices; and Other Stories*, 1
       vol. (Isbister).
       The Fixed Period, 2 vols. (Blackwood).
       Marion Fay, 3 vols. (Chapman & Hall).
       Lord Palmerston, 1 vol. (Isbister).
       Kept in the Dark, 2 vols. (Chatto & Windus).
       (May) Visits Ireland to collect material for a new Irish
       novel.
       (Aug.) Returns to Ireland a second time.
       (2 Oct.) Takes rooms for the winter at Garlant's Hotel,
       Suffolk St., London.
       (3 Nov.) Suffers paralytic stroke.
       (6 Dec.) Dies in nursing home, 34 Welbeck St., London.

1883   *Mr. Scarborough's Family*, 3 vols. (Chatto & Windus).
       The Landleaguers (unfinished), 3 vols. (Chatto & Windus).
       An Autobiography, 2 vols. (Blackwood).

1884   *An Old Man's Love*, 2 vols. (Blackwood).

1923   *The Noble Jilt*, 1 vol. (Constable).

1927   *London Tradesmen*, 1 vol. (Elkin Mathews and Marrat).

1972   *The New Zealander*, 1 vol. (Oxford University Press).

HARRY HEATHCOTE OF GANGOIL

CHAPTER I

GANGOIL

JUST a fortnight before Christmas, 1871,* a young man, twenty-four years of age,* returned home to his dinner about eight o'clock in the evening. He was married, and with him and his wife lived his wife's sister. At that somewhat late hour he walked in among the two young women, and another much older woman, who was preparing the table for dinner. The wife and the wife's sister each had a child in her lap, the elder having seen some fifteen months of its existence, and the younger three months.* 'He has been out since seven, and I don't think he's had a mouthful,' the wife had just said. 'Oh, Harry, you must be half-starved,' she exclaimed, jumping up to greet him, and throwing her arm round his bare neck.

'I'm about whole melted,' he said, as he kissed her. 'In the name of charity give me a nobbler. I did get a bit of damper* and a pannikin of tea up at the German's hut; but I never was so hot or so thirsty in my life. We're going to have it in earnest this time. Old Bates says that when the gum leaves crackle, as they do now, before Christmas, there won't be a blade of grass by the end of February.'*

'I hate old Bates,' said the wife. 'He always prophesies evil, and complains about his rations.'

'He knows more about sheep than any man this side of the Mary,' said her husband.

From all this I trust the reader will understand that the Christmas to which he is introduced is not the Christmas with which he is intimate on this side of the Equator—a Christmas of blazing fires indoors, and of sleet and snow and frost outside—but the Christmas of Australia, in which happy land the Christmas fires are apt to be lighted, or to light themselves, when they are by no means needed.

The young man who had just returned home had on a flannel shirt, a pair of moleskin trousers, and an old straw hat, battered nearly out of all shape. He had no coat, no waistcoat, no braces, and nothing round his neck. Round his waist there was a strap or belt, from the front of which hung a small pouch, and, behind, a knife in a case; and stuck into a loop in the belt made for the purpose there was a small briar-wood pipe. As he dashed his hat off, wiped his brow, and threw himself into a rocking-chair, he certainly was rough to look at; but by all who understood Australian life he would have been taken to be a gentleman. He was a young squatter,* well known west of the Mary river in Queensland.* Harry Heathcote of Gangoil, who owned 30,000 sheep of his own, was a magistrate in those parts,* and able to hold his own among his neighbours, whether rough or gentle; and some neighbours he had very rough, who made it almost necessary that a man should be able to be rough also, on occasions, if he desired to live among them without injury. Heathcote of Gangoil could do all that. Men said of him that he was too imperious, too masterful, too much inclined to think that all things should be made to go as he would have them. Young as he was, he had been altogether his own master since he was of age—and not only his own master, but the master also of all with whom he was brought into contact from day to day. In his life he conversed but seldom with any except those who were dependent on him, nor had he done so for the last three years. At an age at which young men at home are still subject to pastors and masters, he had sprung at once into patriarchal power, and, being a man determined to thrive, had become laborious and thoughtful beyond his years.

Harry Heathcote had been left an orphan, with a small fortune in money, when he was fourteen. For two years after that he had consented to remain quietly at school, but at sixteen he declared his purpose of emigrating. Boys less than himself in stature got above him at school,* and he had not liked it. For a twelvemonth he was opposed by his guardian; but at the end of the year he was fitted forth for the colony. The guardian was not sorry to be quit of him, but prophesied that he would be home again before a year was over. The lad had not returned, and it was now a settled conviction among all who knew him that he would make or mar his fortune in the new land that he had chosen.

He was a tall, well-made young fellow, with fair hair and a good-humoured smile, but ever carrying in his countenance marks of what his enemies called pigheadedness, his acquaintances obstinacy, and those who loved him, firmness. His acquaintances were, perhaps, right, for he certainly was obstinate. He would take no man's advice, he would submit himself to no man, and in the conduct of his own business preferred to trust to his own insight rather than to the experience of others. It would sometimes occur that he had to pay heavily for his obstinacy. But, on the other hand, the lessons which he learned, he learned thoroughly. And he was kept right in his trade by his own indefatigable industry. That trade was the growth of wool. He was a breeder of sheep on a Queensland sheep-run, and his flocks ran far afield over a vast territory of which he was the only lord. His house was near the river Mary, and beyond the river his domain did not extend; but around him on his own side of the river he could ride for ten miles in each direction without getting off his own pastures. He was master, as far as his mastership went, of 120,000 acres*—almost an English county—and it was the pride of his heart to put his foot off his own territory as seldom as possible. He sent his wool annually down to Brisbane, and received his stores, tea and sugar, flour and brandy, boots, clothes, tobacco, etc., once or twice a year from thence. But the

traffic did not require his own presence at the city. So
self-contained was the working of the establishment that he
was never called away by his business unless he went to
see some lot of highly-bred sheep which he might feel
disposed to buy; and as for pleasure, it had come to be
altogether beyond the purpose of his life to go in quest of
that. When the work of the day was over, he would lie at
his length upon rugs in the verandah, with a pipe in his
mouth, while his wife sat over him reading a play of
Shakespeare or the last novel that had come to them from
England.*

He had married a fair girl, the orphan daughter of a
bankrupt squatter whom he had met in Sydney, and had
brought her and her sister into the Queensland bush with
him. His wife idolized him. His sister-in-law, Kate Daly,
loved him dearly—as she had cause to do for he had proved
himself to be a very brother to her—but she feared him also
somewhat. The people about the Mary said that she was
fairer and sweeter to look at, even than the elder sister. Mrs
Heathcote was the taller of the two, and the larger-featured.
She certainly was the higher in intellect, and the fittest to
be the mistress of such an establishment as that at Gangoil.

When he had washed his hands and face, and had
swallowed the very copious but weak allowance of brandy
and water which his wife mixed for him, he took the eldest
boy on his lap and fondled him.

'By George!' he said, 'old fellow, you shan't be a squatter.'

'Why not, Harry?' asked his wife.

'Because I don't want him to break his heart every day
of his life.'

'Are you always breaking yours? I thought your heart
was pretty well hardened now.'

'When a man talks of his heart you and Kate are thinking
of loves and doves, of course.'

'I wasn't thinking of loves and doves, Harry,' said Kate.
'I was thinking how very hot it must have been to-day. We

could only bear it in the verandah by keeping the blinds always wet. I don't wonder that you were troubled.'

'That comes from heaven or Providence, or from something that one knows to be unassailable, and therefore one can put up with it. Even if one gets a sun-stroke, one does not complain. The sun has a right to be there, and is no interloper, like a free-selector.* I can't understand why free-selectors and musquitoes should have been introduced into the arrangements of the world.'

'I s'pose the poor must live somewheres, and 'squiters, too,' said Mrs Growler, the old maid-servant, as she put a boiled leg of mutton on the table. 'Now, Mr Harry, if you're hungered there's something for you to eat, in spite of the free-selectors.'

'Mrs. Growler,' said the master, 'excuse me for saying that you jump to conclusions.'

'My jumping is pretty well nigh done,' said the old woman.

'By no means. I find that old people can jump quite as briskly as young. You have rebuked me under the impression that I was grudging something to the poor. Let me explain to you that a free-selector may be, and very often is, a rich man. He whom I had in my mind is not a poor man, though I won't swear but what he will be before a year is over.'

'I know who you mean, Mr Harry; you mean the Medlicots. A very nice gentleman is Mr Medlicot, and a very nice old lady is Mrs Medlicot. And a deal of good they're going to do by all accounts.'

'Now, Mrs Growler, that will do,' said the wife.

The dinner consisted of a boiled leg of mutton, a large piece of roast beef, potatoes, onions, and an immense pot of tea. No glasses were even put upon the table. The two ladies had dressed for dinner, and were bright and pretty as they would have been in a country-house at home; but Harry Heathcote had sat down just as he had entered the room.

'I know you are tired to death,' said his wife, 'when I see you eat your dinner like that.'

'It isn't being tired, Mary; I'm not particularly tired. But I must be off again in about an hour.'

'Out again to-night?'

'Yes, indeed.'

'On horseback?'

'How else? Old Bates and Mickey are in their saddles still. I don't want to have my fences burned as soon as they're put up. It's a ticklish thing to think that a spark of fire anywhere about the place might ruin me, and to know at the same time that every man about the run, and every swagsman that passes along, have matches in their pockets. There isn't a pipe lighted on Gangoil this time of the year that mightn't make a beggar of you and me. That's another reason why I wouldn't have the young'un a squatter.'

'I declare I think that squatters have more trouble than any people in the world,' said Kate Daly.

'Free-selectors have their own troubles too, Kate,' said he.

It must be explained, as we go on, that Heathcote felt that he had received a great and peculiar grievance from the hands of one Medlicot, a stranger who had lately settled near him; and that this last remark referred to a somewhat favourable opinion which had been expressed about the stranger by the two ladies. It was a little unfair, as having been addressed specially to Kate—intending, as it did, to imply that Kate had better consider the matter well before she allowed her opinion of the stranger to become dangerously favourable—for in truth she had said no more than her sister.

'The Medlicots' troubles will never trouble me, Harry,' she said.

'I hope not, Kate; nor mine either more than we can help.'

'But they do,' said Mary. 'They trouble me, and her too, very much.'

'A man's back should be broad enough to bear all that for himself,' said Harry. 'I get ashamed of myself when I grumble; and yet one seems to be surly if one doesn't say what one's thinking.'

'I hope you'll always tell me what you're thinking, dear.'

'Well, I suppose I shall—till this fellow is old enough to be talked to, and to be made to bear the burden of his father's care.'

'By that time, Harry, you will have got rich, and we shall all be in England—shan't we?'

'I don't know about being rich, but we shall have been free-selected off Gangoil. Now, Mrs Growler, we've done dinner, and I'll have a pipe before I make another start. Is Jacko in the kitchen? Send him through to me on to the verandah.'

Gangoil was decidedly in the bush; according to common Australian parlance, all sheep stations are in the bush, even though there should not be a tree or shrub within sight. They who live away from the towns live a 'bush life'. Small towns, as they grow up, are called bush towns—as we talk of country towns. The 'bush', indeed, is the country generally. But the Heathcotes lived absolutely and actually in the bush. There are Australian pastures which consist of plains on which not a tree is to be seen for miles; but others are forests, so far extending that their limits are almost unknown. Gangoil was surrounded by forest, in some places so close as to be impervious to men and almost to animals, in which the undergrowth was thick and tortuous and almost platted, through which no path could be made without an axe,* but of which the greater portions were open, without any underwood, between which the sheep could wander at their will, and men could ride, with a sparse surface of coarse grass, which after rain would be luxuriant, but in hot weather would be scorched down to the ground. At such times—and those times were by far the more common—a stranger would wonder where the sheep would find their feed. Immediately round the house, or station, as it was called, about one hundred acres had been cleared, or nearly cleared, with a few trees left here and there for ornament or shade. Further afield, but still round the home quarters, the trees had been destroyed, the run of the sap having been stopped by 'ringing' the bark; but they still stood like troops of skeletons,* and would stand, very ugly to look at, till they fell in the course of nature by reason of their own rottenness. There was a man always at work about the place—Boscobel he was called— whose sole business was to destroy the timber after this fashion, so that the air might get through to the grasses, and that the soil might be relieved from the burden of nurturing the forest trees.

For miles around, the domain was divided into paddocks, as they were there called; but these were so large that a stranger might wander in one of them for a day and never discover that he was enclosed. There were five or six paddocks on the Gangoil run, each of which comprised over ten thousand acres, and as all the land was undulating, and as the timber was around you everywhere, one paddock was exactly like another. The scenery in itself was fine, for the trees were often large, and here and there rocky knolls would crop up, and there were broken crevices in the ground; but it was all alike. A stranger would wonder that any one straying from the house should find his way back to it. There were sundry bush houses here and there, and the so-called road to the coast from the wide pastoral districts farther west passed across the run; but these roads and tracks would travel hither and thither, new tracks being opened from time to time by the heavy wool drays and store waggons, as in wet weather the ruts on the old tracks would become insurmountable.*

The station itself was certainly very pretty. It consisted of a cluster of cottages, each of which possessed a ground floor only. No such luxury as stairs was known at Gangoil.

It stood about half a mile from the Mary river, on the edge
of a creek which ran into it. The principal edifice, that in
which the Heathcotes lived, contained only one sitting-
room, and a bedroom on each side of it; but in truth there
was another room, very spacious, in which the family really
passed their time; and this was the verandah which ran
along the front and two ends of the house.* It was twelve
feet broad, and of course of great length. Here were
clustered the rocking-chairs and sofas and work-tables, and
very often the cradle of the family. Here stood Mrs Heathcote's sewing-machine; and here the master would sprawl
at his length, while his wife, or his wife's sister, read to him.
It was here, in fact, that they lived, having a parlour simply
for their meals. Behind the main edifice there stood, each
apart, various buildings, forming an irregular quadrangle.
The kitchen came first, with a small adjacent chamber, in
which slept the Chinese man cook, Sing Sing, as he had
come to be called; then the cottage, consisting also of three
rooms and a small verandah, in which lived Harry's superintendent, commonly known as Old Bates—a man who had
been a squatter once himself, and, having lost his all in bad
times, now worked for a small salary. In the cottage, two
of the rooms were devoted to hospitality when, as was not
unusual, guests known or unknown came the way; and here
Harry himself would sleep, if the entertainment of other
ladies crowded the best apartments. Then at the back of
the quadrangle was the store—perhaps of all the buildings
the most important. In here was kept a kind of shop, which
was supposed, according to an obsolete rule, to be open
for custom for half a day twice a week. The exigencies of
the station did not allow of this regularity; but after some
fashion the shop was maintained. Tea was to be bought
there, and sugar, tobacco, and pickles, jam, nails, boots,
hats, flannel shirts, and moleskin trousers. Anybody who
came might buy; but the intention was to provide the
station hands, who would otherwise have had to go or send

thirty miles for the supply of their wants. Very little money was taken here—generally none—but the quantity of pickles, jam, and tobacco sold was great. The men would consume large quantities of these bush delicacies, and the cost would be deducted from their wages. The tea and sugar, and flour also, was given out weekly as rations—so much a week—and meat was supplied to them after the same fashion; for it was the duty of this young autocratic patriarch to find provisions for all who were employed around him. For such luxuries as jam and tobacco the men paid themselves. On the fourth side of the quadrangle was a rough coach-house, and rougher stables. The carriage part of the establishment consisted of two 'buggies'—so called always in the bush—open carriages on four wheels,* one of which was intended to hold two, and the other four sitters. A Londoner looking at them would have declared them to be hopeless ruins; but Harry Heathcote still made wonderful journeys in them, taking care generally that the wheels were sound, and using ropes for the repair of dilapidations. The stables were almost unnecessary, as the horses, of which the supply at Gangoil was very large, roamed in the horse-paddock—a comparatively small enclosure, containing not above three or four hundred acres—and were driven up as they were wanted. One horse was always kept close at home with which to catch the others; but this horse, for handiness, was generally hitched to a post outside the kitchen door. Harry was proud of his horses, and was sometimes heard to say that few men in England had a lot of thirty at hand as he had, out of which so many would be able to carry a man eighty miles in eight hours at a moment's notice. But his stable arrangements would not have commanded respect in the 'Shires'. The animals were never groomed, never fed, and most of them never shod. They lived upon grass, and, as he always said, 'cut their own bread and butter' for themselves.

Gangoil was certainly very pretty. The verandah was covered in with striped blinds, so that when the sun shone hot, or when the rains fell heavily, or when the musquitoes were more than usually troublesome, there might be something of the protection of an enclosed room. Up all the posts there were flowering creepers, which covered the front with greenery even when the flowers were wanting. From the front of the house down to the creek there was a pleasant falling garden—heartbreaking, indeed, in regard to vegetables, for the opossums always came first, and they who followed the opossums got but little. But the garden gave a pleasant homelike look to the place, and was very dear to Harry, who was perhaps indifferent in regard to peas and tomatoes. Harry Heathcote was very proud of the place, for he had made it all himself, having pulled down a wretched barrack that he had found there. But he was far prouder of his wool-shed, which he had also built, and which he regarded as first and foremost among wool-sheds in those parts. By-and-by we shall be called on to visit the wool-shed. Though Heathcote had done all this for Gangoil, it must be understood that the vast extent of territory over which his sheep ran was by no means his own property. He was simply the tenant of the Crown, paying a rent computed at so much a sheep. He had indeed purchased the ground on which his house stood, but this he had done simply to guard himself against other purchasers. These other purchasers were the bane of his existence—the one great sorrow which, as he said, broke his heart.

While he was speaking, a rough-looking lad, about sixteen years of age, came through the parlour to the verandah, dressed very much like his master, but unwashed, uncombed, a..d with that wild look which falls upon those who wander about the Australian plains, living a nomad life. This was Jacko—so-called, and no one knew him by any other name—a lad whom Heathcote had picked up about six months since, and who had become a favourite.

'The old woman says as you was wanting me?' suggested Jacko.

'Going to be fine to-night, Jacko?'

Jacko went to the edge of the verandah and looked up to the sky.

'My word! little squall a coming!'* he said.

'I wish it would come from ten thousand buckets!' said the master.

'No buckets at all,' said Jacko. 'Want the horses, master?'

'Of course I want the horses, and I want you to come with me. There are two horses saddled there; I'll ride Hamlet.'

CHAPTER II

A NIGHT'S RIDE

HARRY jumped from the ground, kissed his wife, called her 'old girl' and told her to be happy, and got on his horse at the garden gate. Both the ladies came off the verandah to see him start.

'It's as dark as pitch,' said Kate Daly.

'That's because you have just come out of the light.'

'But it is dark—quite dark. You won't be late, will you?' said the wife.

'I can't be very early as it's near ten now. I shall be back about twelve.' So saying, he broke at once into a gallop and vanished into the night, his young groom scampering after him.

'Why should he go out now?' Kate said to her sister.

'He is afraid of fire.'

'But he can't prevent the fires by riding about in the dark. I suppose the fires come from the heat.'

'He thinks they come from enemies, and he has heard something. One wretched man may do so much when everything is dried to tinder. I do so wish it would rain.'

The night in truth was very dark. It was now midsummer, at which time with us the days are so long that the coming of the one almost catches the departure of its predecessor. But Gangoil was not far outside the tropics, and there were no long summer nights. The heat was intense; but there was a low soughing wind, which seemed to moan among the trees without moving them. As they crossed the little home enclosure and the horse-paddock the track was just visible, the trees being dead and the spaces open. About half a mile from the house, while they were still in the horse-paddock, Harry turned from the track, and Jacko, of course, turned with him.

'You can sit your horse jumping, Jacko?' he asked.

'My word! jump like glory!' answered Jacko.

He was soon tried. Harry rode at the bush fence, which was not, indeed, much of a fence, made of logs lengthways and crossways, about three feet and a half high, and went over it. Jacko followed him, rushing his horse at the leap, losing his seat, and almost falling over the animal's shoulders as he came to the ground.

'My word!' said Jacko, just saving himself by a scramble; 'who ever saw the like of that?'

'Why don't you sit in your saddle, you stupid young duffer?'

'Sit in my saddle! Why don't he jump proper? Well, you go on. I don't know that I'm a duffer. Duffer, indeed!* My word!'

Heathcote had turned to the left, leaving the track, which was indeed the main road towards the nearest town and the coast, and was now pushing on through the forest with no pathway at all to guide him. To ordinary eyes the attempt to steer any course would have been hopeless. But an Australian squatter, if he have any well-grounded claim to the character of a bushman, has eyes which are not ordinary, and he has, probably, nurtured within himself, unconsciously, topographical instincts which are unintelligible to the inhabitants of cities. Harry, too, was near his own home, and went forward through the thick gloom without a doubt, Jacko following him faithfully. In about half an hour they came to another fence, but now it was too absolutely dark for jumping. Harry had not seen it till he was close to it, and then he pulled up his horse.

'My word! why don't you jump away, Mr Harry? Who's a duffer now?'

'Hold your tongue, or I'll put my whip across your back. Get down and help me pull a log away. The horses couldn't see where to put their feet.'

Jacko did as he was bid, and worked hard, but still grumbled at having been called a duffer. The animals were quickly led over, the logs were replaced, and the two were again galloping through the forest. 'I thought you were making for the wool-shed,' said Jacko.

'We're eight miles beyond the wool-shed,' said Harry. They had now crossed another paddock, and had come to the extreme fence on the run. The Gangoil pastures extended much farther, but in that direction had not as yet been enclosed. Here they both got off their horses and walked along the fence till they came to an opening—with a slip panel, or moveable bars—which had been Heathcote's intended destination. 'Hold the horses, Jacko, till I come back,' he said.

Jacko, when alone, nothing daunted by the darkness or solitude, seated himself on the top rail, took out a pipe, and struck a match. When the tobacco was ignited he dropped the match on the dry grass at his feet, and a little flame instantly sprang up. The boy waited a few seconds till the flames began to run, and then, putting his feet together on the ground, stamped out the incipient fire. 'My word!' said Jacko to himself; 'it's easy done, any way.'

Harry went on to the left for about half a mile, and then stood leaning against the fence. It was very dark, but he was now looking over into an enclosure which had been altogether cleared of trees, and which, as he knew well, had been cultivated and was covered with sugar-canes. Where he stood he was not distant above a quarter of a mile from the river, and the field before him ran down to the banks. This was the selected land of Giles Medlicot—two years since a portion of his own run, which had now been purchased from the Government—for the loss of which he had received and was entitled to receive no compensation. And the matter was made worse for him by the fact that the interloper had come between him and the river. But he was not standing here near midnight merely to exercise his wrath by straining his eyes through the darkness at his neighbour's crops. He put his finger into his mouth to wet it, and then held it up that he might discover which way the light breath of wind was coming. There was still the low moan to be heard continually through the forest, and yet not a leaf seemed to be moved.

After a while he thought he caught a sound, and put his ear down to the ground. He distinctly heard a footstep, and, rising up, walked quickly towards the spot whence the noise came.

'Who's that?' he said, as he saw the figure of a man standing on his side of the fence, and leaning against it, with a pipe in his mouth.

'Who are you?' replied the man on the fence. 'My name is Medlicot.'

'Oh, Mr Medlicot, is it?'

'Is that Mr Heathcote? Good night, Mr Heathcote. You are going about at a late hour of the night.'

'I have to go about early and late; but I ain't later than you.'

'I'm close at home,' said Medlicot.

'I am, at any rate, on my own run,' said Harry.

'You mean to say that I am trespassing,' said the other; 'because I can very soon jump back over the fence.'

'I didn't mean that at all, Mr Medlicot; anybody is welcome on my run, night or day, who knows how to behave himself.'

'I hope I'm included in that list.'

'Just so—of course. Considering the state that everything is in, and all the damage that a fire would do, I rather wish that people would be a little more careful about smoking.'

'My canes, Mr Heathcote, would burn quite as quickly as your grass.'

'It is not only the grass. I've a hundred miles of fencing on the run, which is as dry as tinder; not to talk of the station and the wool-shed.'

'They shan't suffer from my neglect, Mr Heathcote.'

'You have men about who mayn't be so careful. The wind, such as it is, is coming right across from your place. If there were light enough, I could show you three or four patches where there has been fire within half a mile of this spot. There was a log burning there for two or three days, not long ago, which was lighted by one of your men.'

'That was a fortnight since. There was no heat then, and the men were boiling their kettle. I spoke about it.'

'A log like that, Mr Medlicot, will burn for weeks sometimes. I'll tell you fairly what I'm afraid of. There's a man with you whom I turned out of the shed last shearing, and I think he might put a match down—not by accident.'

'You mean Nokes. As far as I know, he's a decent man. You wouldn't have me not employ a man just because you had dismissed him?'

'Certainly not—that is, I shouldn't think of dictating to you about such a thing.'

'Well, no, Mr Heathcote, I suppose not. Nokes has got to earn his bread though you did dismiss him. I don't know that he's not as honest a man as you or I.'

'If so, there's three of us very bad—that's all, Mr Medlicot. Good night—and if you'll trouble yourself to look after the ash of your tobacco it might be the saving of me and all I have.' So saying, he turned round, and made his way back to the horses.

Medlicot had placed himself on the fence during the interview, and he still kept his seat. Of course he was now thinking of the man who had just left him, whom he declared to himself to be an ignorant, prejudiced, ill-conditioned cur. 'I believe in his heart he thinks that I'm going to set fire to his run,' he said almost aloud. 'And because he grows wool he thinks himself above everybody in the colony. He occupies thousands of acres, and employs three or four men. I till about two hundred, and maintain thirty

families.* But he is such a pig that he can't understand all
that; and he thinks that I must be something low because
I've bought with my own money a bit of land which never
belonged to him, and which he couldn't use.' Such was the
nature of Giles Medlicot's soliloquy as he sat swinging his
legs, and still smoking his pipe, on the fence which divided
his sugar-canes from the other young man's run.

And Harry Heathcote uttered his soliloquy also. 'I
wouldn't swear that he wouldn't do it himself, after all;'
meaning that he almost suspected that Medlicot himself
would be an incendiary. To him, in his way of thinking, a
man who would take advantage of the law to buy a bit of
another man's land—or become a free-selector, as the term
goes—was a public enemy, and might be presumed capable
of any iniquity. It was all very well for the girls—meaning
his wife and sister-in-law—to tell him that Medlicot had
the manners of a gentleman, and had come of decent
people. Women were always soft enough to be taken by
soft hands, a good-looking face, and a decent coat. This
Medlicot went about dressed like a man in the towns,
exhibiting, as Harry thought, a contemptible, unmanly
finery. Of what use was it to tell him that Medlicot was a
gentleman? What Harry knew was, that, since Medlicot had
come, he had lost his sheep, that the heads of three or four
had been found buried on Medlicot's side of his run, and
that if he dismissed 'a hand' Medlicot employed him—a
proceeding which, in Harry Heathcote's aristocratic
and patriarchal views of life, was altogether ungentleman-
like. How were the 'hands' to be kept in their place if one
employer of labour did not back up another?

He had been warned to be on his guard against fire. The
warnings had hardly been explicit, but yet had come in a
shape which made him unable to ignore them. Old Bates,
whom he trusted implicitly, and who was a man of very
few words, had told him to be on his guard. The German,
at whose hut he had been in the morning, Karl Bender by

name, and a servant of his own, had told him that there would be fire about before long. 'Why should any one want to ruin me?' Harry had asked. 'Did I ever wrong a man of a shilling?' The German had learned to know his young master, had made his way through the crust of his master's character, and was prepared to be faithful at all points—though he, too, could have quarrelled, and have avenged himself, had it not chanced that he had come to the point of loving instead of hating his employer.

'You like too much to be governor over all,' said the German,* as he stooped over the fire in his own hut in his anxiety to boil the water for Heathcote's tea.

'Somebody must be governor, or everything would go to the devil!' said Harry.

'Dat's true; only fellows don't like be made feel it,' said the German. 'Nokes, he was made feel it when you put him over de gate.'

But neither would Bates nor the German express absolute suspicion of any man. That Medlicot's 'hands' at the sugar-mill were stealing his sheep, Harry thought that he knew; but that was comparatively a small affair, and he would not have pressed it, as he was without absolute evidence. And even he had a feeling that it would be unwise to increase the anger felt against himself—at any rate, during the present heats.

Jacko had his pipe still alight when Heathcote returned. 'You young monkey,' said he, 'have you been using matches?'

'Why not, Mr Harry? Don't the grass burn ready, Mr Harry? My word!' Then Jacko stooped down, lit another match, and showed Heathcote the burned patch.

'Was it so when we came?' Harry asked, with emotion. Jacko, still kneeling on the ground, and holding the lighted match in his hand, shook his head and tapped his breast, indicating that he had burned the grass. 'You dropped the match by accident?'

'My word, no! Did it o' purpose to see. It's all just one as gunpowder, Mr Harry.'

Harry got on his horse without a word, and rode away through the forest, taking a direction different from that by which he had come, and the boy followed him. He was by no means certain that this young fellow might not turn against him; but it had been a part of his theory to make no difference to any man because of such fears. If he could make the men around him respect him, then they would treat him well; but they could never be brought to respect him by flattery. He was very nearly right in his views of men, and would have been right altogether could he have seen accurately what justice demanded for others as well as for himself. As far as the intention went, he was minded to be just to every man.

It seemed, as they were riding, that the heat grew fiercer and fiercer. Though there was still the same moaning sound, there was not a breath of air. They had now got upon a track very well known to Heathcote, which led up from the river to the wool-shed, and so on to the station, and they had turned homewards. When they were near the wool-shed, suddenly there fell a heavy drop or two of rain. Harry stopped, and turned his face upwards, when, in a moment, the whole heavens above them and the forest around were illumined by a flash of lightning so near them that it made each of them start in his saddle, and made the horses shudder in every limb. Then came the roll of thunder immediately over their heads, and, with the thunder, rain so thick and fast that Harry's 'ten thousand buckets' seemed to be emptied directly over their heads.

'God A'mighty has put out the fires now,' said Jacko.

Harry paused for a moment, feeling the rain through to his bones, for he had nothing on over his shirt, and rejoicing in it. 'Yes,' he said, 'we may go to bed for a week, and let the grass grow and the creeks fill, and the earth cool. Half an hour like this over the whole run, and there won't be a dry stick on it.' As they went on, the horses splashed through the water. It seemed as though a deluge were falling, and that already the ground beneath their feet were becoming a lake.

'We might have too much of this, Jacko.'

'My word, yes!'

'I don't want to have the Mary flooded again.'

'My word, no!'

But by the time they reached the wool-shed it was over. From the first drop to the last there had hardly been a space of twenty minutes. But still there was a noise of waters as the little streams washed hither and thither to their destined courses, and still the horses splashed, and still there was the feeling of an incipient deluge. When they reached the wool-shed, Harry again got off his horse, and Jacko, dismounting also, hitched the two animals to the post, and followed his master into the building. Harry struck a wax match, and, holding it up, strove to look round the building by the feeble light which it shed. It was a remarkable edifice, built in the shape of a great T, open at the sides, with a sharp-pitched timber roof covered with felt, which came down within four feet of the ground. It was calculated to hold about four hundred sheep at a time, and was divided into pens of various sizes, partitioned off for various purposes. If Harry Heathcote was sure of anything he was sure that his wool-shed was the best that had ever been built in this district.

'By Jimini! what's that?' said Jacko.

'Did you hear anything?' Jacko pointed with his finger down the centre walk of the shed, and Harry, striking another match as he went, rushed forward. But the match was out as soon as ignited, and gave no glimmer of light. Nevertheless he saw, or thought that he saw, the figure of a man escaping out of the open end of the shed. The place itself was black as midnight, but the space beyond was clear of trees, and the darkness outside, being a few shades lighter than within the building, allowed something of the outline of a figure to be visible; and, as the man escaped, the sounds of his footsteps were audible enough. Harry called to him, but of course received no answer. Had he pursued him he would have been obliged to cross sundry rails, which would have so delayed him as to give him no chance of success. 'I knew there was a fellow about,' he said; 'one of our own men would not have run like that.' Jacko shook his head, but did not speak. 'He got in here for shelter out of the rain, but he was doing no good about the place.' Jacko again shook his head. 'I wonder who he was?'

Jacko came up and whispered in his ear, 'Bill Nokes.'

'You couldn't see him.'

'Seed the drag of his leg.' Now it was well known that the man Nokes had injured some of his muscles, and habitually dragged one foot after another.

'I don't think you could have been sure of him by such a glimpse as that.'

'May be not,' said the boy, 'only I'm sure as sure.'

Harry Heathcote said not another word, but, getting again upon his horse, galloped home. It was past one when he reached the station, but the two girls were waiting up for him, and at once began to condole with him because he was wet.

'Wet!' said Harry; 'if you could only know how much I prefer things being wet to dry just at present! But give Jacko some supper. I must keep that young fellow in good humour if I can.'

So Jacko had half a loaf of bread, and a small pot of jam, and a large jug of cold tea provided for him, in the enjoyment of which luxuries he did not seem to be in the least impeded by the fact that he was wet through to the skin. Harry Heathcote had another nobbler—being only the second in the day—and then went to bed.

CHAPTER III

MEDLICOT'S MILL

As Harry had said, they might all now lie in bed for a day or two. The rain had set aside for the time the necessity for that urgent watchfulness which kept all hands on the station hard at work during the great heat. There was not, generally, much rest during the year at Gangoil. Lambing in April and May, washing and shearing in September, October, and November, with the fear of fires and the necessary precautions in December and January, did not leave more than sufficient intervals for looking after the water-dams, making and mending fences, procuring stores, and attending to the ailments of the flocks. No man worked harder than the young squatter. But now there had suddenly come a day or two of rest—rest from work which was not of itself productive, but only remedial, and which, therefore, was not begrudged.

But it soon was apparent that the rest could be only for a day or two. The rain had fallen as from ten thousand buckets, but it had fallen only for a space of minutes. On the following morning the thirsty earth had apparently swallowed all the flood. The water in the creek beneath the house stood two feet higher than it had done, and Harry, when he visited the dams round the run, found that they were full to overflowing, and the grasses were already springing, so quick is the all but tropical growth of the country. They might be safe, perhaps, for eight-and-forty hours. Fire would run only when the ground was absolutely dry, and when every twig or leaf was a combustible. But during those eight and forty hours there might be comparative ease at Gangoil.

On the day following the night of the ride Mrs Heathcote suggested to her husband that she and Kate should ride over to Medlicot's Mill, as the place was already named, and call on Mrs Medlicot. 'It isn't Christian,' she said, 'for people living out in the bush, as we are, to quarrel with their neighbours just because they are neighbours.'

'Neighbours!' said Harry; 'I don't know any word that there's so much humbug about. The Samaritan was the best neighbour I ever heard of, and he lived a long way off, I take it. Any way, he wasn't a free-selector.'

'Harry, that's profane.'

'Everything I say is wicked. You can go, of course, if you like it. I don't want to quarrel with anybody.'

'Quarrelling is so uncomfortable,' said his wife.

'That's a matter of taste. There are people whom I find it very comfortable to quarrel with. I shouldn't at all like not to quarrel with the Brownbies, and I'm not at all sure it mayn't come to be the same with Mr Giles Medlicot.'

'The Brownbies live by sheep-stealing and horse-stealing.'

'And Medlicot means to live by employing sheep-stealers and horse-stealers. You can go if you like it. You won't want me to go with you. Will you have the buggy?'

But the ladies said that they would ride. The air was cooler now than it had been, and they would like the exercise. They would take Jacko with them to open the slip-rails, and they would be back by seven for dinner. So they started, taking the track by the wool-shed. The wool-shed was about two miles from the station, and Medlicot's Mill was seven miles farther, on the bank of the river.

Mr Giles Medlicot, though at Gangoil he was still spoken of as a new-comer, had already been located for nearly two years on the land which he had purchased immediately on his coming to the colony. He had come out direct from England with the intention of growing sugar, and, whether successful or not in making money, had certainly succeeded in growing crops of sugar-canes and in erecting a mill for crushing them. It probably takes more than two years for a man himself to discover whether he can achieve ultimate success in such an enterprise; and Medlicot was certainly not a man likely to talk much to others of his private concerns. The mill had just been built, and he had lived there himself as soon as a water-tight room had been constructed. It was only within the last three months that he had completed a small cottage residence, and had brought his mother to live with him. Hitherto he had hardly made himself popular. He was not either fish or fowl. The squatters regarded him as an interloper, and as a man holding opinions directly adverse to their own interests—in which they were right. And the small free-selectors, who lived on the labour of their own hands—or, as was said of many of them, by stealing sheep and cattle—knew well that he was not of their class. But Medlicot had gone his way steadfastly, if not happily, and complained aloud to no one in the midst of his difficulties. He had not, perhaps, found the Paradise which he had expected in Queensland, but he had found that he could grow sugar, and, having begun the work, he was determined to go on with it.

Heathcote was his nearest neighbour, and the only man in his own rank of life who lived within twenty miles of him. When he had started his enterprise he had hoped to make this man his friend, not comprehending at first how great a cause for hostility was created by the very purchase of the land. He had been a new-comer from the old country, and, being alone, had desired friendship. He was Harry Heathcote's equal in education, intelligence, and fortune, if not in birth—which surely in the Australian bush need not count for much. He had assumed, when first meeting the squatter, that good fellowship between them, on equal terms, would be acceptable to both; but his overtures had been coldly received. Then he, too, had drawn himself up, had declared that Heathcote was an ignorant ass, and had unconsciously made up his mind to

commence hostilities. It was in this spirit that he had taken
Nokes into his mill—of whose character, had he inquired
about it, he would certainly have heard no good. He had
now brought his mother to Medlicot's Mill. She and the
Gangoil ladies had met each other on neutral ground; and
it was almost necessary that they should either be friends
or absolute enemies. Mrs Heathcote had been aware of this,
and had declared that enmity was horrible.

'Upon my word,' said Harry, 'I sometimes think that
friendship is more so. I suppose I'm fitted for bush life, for
I want to see no one from year's end to year's end but my
own family and my own people.' And yet this young
patriarch in the wilderness was only twenty-four years old,
and had been educated at an English school!

Medlicot's cottage was about a hundred and fifty yards
from the mill, looking down upon the Mary, the banks of
which at this spot were almost precipitous. The site for the
plantation had been chosen because the river afforded the
means of carriage down to the sea, and the mill had been
so constructed that the sugar hogsheads could be lowered
from the buildings into the river-boats. Here Mrs Heathcote
and Kate Daly found the old lady sitting at work, all alone,
in the verandah. She was a handsome old woman, with
grey hair, seventy years of age, with wrinkled face, and a
toothless mouth, but with bright eyes, and with no signs of
the infirmity of age.

'This is gay kind of you to run so far to see an auld
woman,' she said.

Mrs Heathcote declared that they were used to the heat,
and that after the rain the air was pleasant.

'You're two bright lasses, and you're hearty,' she said.
'I'm auld, and just out of Cumberland, and I find it's hot
enough—and I'm no gude at horseback at all. I dinna know
how I'm to get aboot.'

Then Mrs Heathcote explained that there was an excellent track for a buggy all the way to Gangoil.

'Giles is ae telling me that I'm to gang aboot in a bouggey, but I do na feel sure of thae bouggies.'

Mrs Heathcote, of course, praised the country carriages, and the country roads, and the country generally. Tea was brought in, and the old lady was delighted with her guests. Since she had been at the mill, week had followed week, and she had seen no woman's face but that of the uncouth girl who waited upon her.

'Did ye ever see rain like that?' she said, putting up her hands. 'I thought the Lord was sending His clouds down upon us in a lump like.'

Then she told them that some of the men had declared that if it went on like that for two hours the Mary would rise and take the cottage away. Giles, however, had declared that to be trash, as the cottage was twenty feet above the ordinary course of the river.

They were just rising to take their leave when Giles Medlicot himself came in out of the mill. He was a man of good presence, dark, not tall like Heathcote, but stoutly made, with a strongly-marked face, given to frowning much when he was eager, bright-eyed, with a broad forehead— certainly a man to be observed as far as his appearance was concerned. He was dressed much as a gentleman dresses in the country at home, and was therefore accounted to be a fop by Harry Heathcote, who was rarely seen abroad in other garb than that which has been described. Harry was an aristocrat, and hated such innovations in the bush as cloth coats and tweed trousers and neck handkerchiefs.

Medlicot had been full of wrath against his neighbour all the morning. There had been a tone in Heathcote's voice when he gave his parting warning as to the fire in Medlicot's pipe, which the sugar-grower had felt to be intentionally insolent. Nothing had been said which could be openly resented, but offence had surely been intended; and then he had remembered that his mother had been already some months at the mill, and that no mark of neighbourly courtesy had been shown to her. The Heathcotes had, he thought, chosen to assume themselves to be superior to him and his, and to treat him as though he had been some labouring man who had saved money enough to purchase a bit of land for himself. He was, therefore, astonished to find the two young ladies sitting with his mother on the very day after such an interview as that of the preceding night.

'The leddies from Gangoil, Giles, have been guid enough to ride over and see me,' said his mother.

Medlicot, of course, shook hands with them, and expressed his sense of their kindness, but he did it awkwardly. He soon, however, declared his purpose of riding part of the way back with them.

'Mr Heathcote must have been very wet last night,' he said, when they were on horseback, addressing himself to Kate Daly rather than to her sister.

'Indeed he was, wet to the skin; were you not?'

'I saw him at about eleven, before the rain began. I was close home, and just escaped. He must have been under it all. Does he often go about the run in that way at night?'

'Only when he's afraid of fires,' said Kate.

'Is there much to be afraid of? I don't suppose that anybody can be so wicked as to wish to burn the grass.'

Then the ladies took upon themselves to explain. 'The fires might be caused from negligence or trifling accidents, or might possibly come from the unaided heat of the sun—or there might be enemies.'

'My word, yes; enemies, rather!' said Jacko, who was riding close behind, and who had no idea of being kept out of the conversation merely because he was a servant.

Medlicot, turning round, looked at the lad, and asked who were the enemies.

'Free-selectors,' said Jacko.

'I'm a free-selector,' said Medlicot.

'Did not jist mean you,' said Jacko.

'Jacko, you'd better hold your tongue,' said Mrs. Heath-cote.

'Hold my tongue! My word! Well, you go on.'*

Medlicot came as far as the wool-shed, and then said that he would return. He had thoroughly enjoyed his ride. Kate Daly was bright, and pretty, and winning; and in the bush, when a man has not seen a lady perhaps for months, brightness and prettiness and winning ways have a double charm. To ride with fair women over turf, through a forest—with a woman who may perhaps some day be wooed—can be a matter of indifference only to a very lethargic man. Giles Medlicot was by no means lethargic. He owned to himself that though Heathcote was a pig-headed ass, the ladies were very nice, and he thought that the pig-headed ass, in choosing one of them for himself, had by no means taken the nicest.

'You'll never find your way back,' said Kate, 'if you've not been here before.'

'I never was here before, and I suppose I must find my way back.'

Then he was urged to come on and dine at Gangoil, with a promise that Jacko should return with him in the evening. But this he would not do. Heathcote was a pig-headed ass, who possibly regarded him as an incen-diary, simply because he had bought some land. This boy of Heathcote's, whose services had been offered to him, had not scrupled to tell him to his face that he was to be regarded as an enemy. Much as he liked the company of Kate Daly, he could not go to the house of that stupid, arrogant, pig-headed young squatter.

'I'm not such a bad bushman but what I can find my way to the river,' he said.

'Find it blindful!' said Jacko, who did not relish the idea of going back to Medlicot's Mill as guide to another man. There was a weakness in the idea that such aid could be necessary, which was revolting to Jacko's sense of bush independence.

They were standing on their horses at the entrance to the wool-shed as they discussed the point, when suddenly Harry himself appeared out of the building. He came up and shook hands with Medlicot, with sufficient courtesy, but hardly with cordiality, and then asked his wife as to her ride.

'We have been very jolly, haven't we, Kate? Of course it has been hot, but everything is not so frightfully parched as it was before the rain. As Mr Medlicot has come back so far with us, we want him to come on and dine.'

'Pray do, Mr Medlicot,' said Harry. But again the tone of his voice was not sufficiently hearty to satisfy the man who was invited.

'Thanks, no; I think I'll hardly do that. Good-night, Mrs Heathcote, good-night, Miss Daly;' and the two ladies immediately perceived that his voice, which had hitherto been pleasant in their ears, had ceased to be cordial.

'I'm very glad he has gone back,' said Heathcote.

'Why do you say so, Harry? You are not given to be inhospitable, and why should you grudge me and Kate the rare pleasure of seeing a strange face?'

'I'll tell you why. It's not about him at this moment; but I've been disturbed. Jacko! go on to the station, and say we're coming. Do you hear me? Go on at once!'

Then Jacko, somewhat unwillingly, galloped off towards the house.

'Get off your horses, and come in here!'

He helped the two ladies from their saddles, and they all went into the wool-shed, Harry leading the way. In one of the side pens, immediately under the roof, there was a large heap of leaves, the outside portion of which was at present damp, for the rain had beaten in upon it, but which had been as dry as tinder when collected; and there was a row or ridge of mixed brush-wood and leaves so constructed as to form a line from the grass outside on to the heap.

'The fellow who did that was an ass,' said Harry; 'a greater ass than I should have taken him to be, not to have known that if he could have gotten the grass to burn outside, the wool-shed must have gone without all that preparation. But there isn't much difficulty now in seeing what the fellow has intended.'

'Was it for a fire?' asked Kate.

'Of course it was. He wouldn't have been contented with the grass and fences, but wanted to make sure of the shed also. He'd have come to the house and burned us in our beds, only a fellow like that is too much of a coward to run the risk of being seen.'

'But, Harry, why didn't he light it when he'd done it?' said Mrs Heathcote.

'Because the Almighty sent the rain at the very moment,' said Harry, striking the top rail of one of the pens with his fist. 'I'm not much given to talk about Providence, but this looks like it; does it not?'

'He might have put a match in at the moment?'

'Rain or no rain? Yes, he might. But he was interrupted by more than the rain. I got into the shed, myself, just at the moment—I and Jacko. It was last night, when the rain was pouring. I heard the man, and, dark as was the night, I saw his figure as he fled away.'

'You didn't know him,' said Miss Daly.

'But that boy, who has the eyes of a cat, he knew him.'

'Jacko?'

'Jacko knew him by his gait. I should have hardly wanted any one to tell me who it was. I could have named the man at once, but for the fear of doing an injustice.'

'And who was it?'

'Our friend Medlicot's prime favourite and new factotum, Mr William Nokes. Mr William Nokes is the gentleman who intends to burn us all out of house and home, and Mr

Medlicot is the gentleman whose pleasure it is to keep Mr Nokes in the neighbourhood.'

The two women stood awestruck for a moment, but a sense of justice prevailed upon the wife to speak.

'That may be all true,' she said. 'Perhaps it is as you say about that man. But you would not therefore think that Mr. Medlicot knows anything about it?'

'It would be impossible,' said Kate.

'I have not accused him,' said Harry; 'but he knows that the man was dismissed, and yet keeps him about the place. Of course he is responsible.'

CHAPTER IV

HARRY HEATHCOTE'S APPEAL

FOR the first mile between the wool-shed and the house Heathcote and the two ladies rode without saying a word. There was something so terrible in the reality of the danger which encompassed them that they hardly felt inclined to discuss it. Harry's dislike to Medlicot was quite a thing apart. That some one had intended to burn down the wool-shed, and had made preparation for doing so, was as apparent to the women as to him; and the man who had been baulked by a shower of rain in his first attempt might soon find an opportunity for a second. Harry was well aware that even Jacko's assertion could not be taken as evidence against the man whom he suspected. In all probability no further attempt would be made upon the wool-shed; but a fire on some distant part of the run would be much more injurious to him than the mere burning of a building. The fire that might ruin him would be one which should get ahead before it was seen, and scour across the ground, consuming the grass down to the very roots over thousands of acres, and destroying fencing over many miles. Such fires pass on, leaving the standing trees unscathed, avoiding even the scrub, which is too moist with the sap of life for consumption, but licking up with fearful rapidity everything that the sun has dried. He could watch the wool-shed and house, but with no possible care could he so watch the whole run as to justify him in feeling security. There need be no preparation of leaves; a match thrown loosely on the ground would do it; and, in regard to a match so thrown, it would be impossible to prove a guilty intention.

'Ought we not to have dispersed the heap?' said Mrs Heathcote at last.

The minds of all of them were full of the matter, but these were the first words spoken.

'I'll leave it as it is,' said Harry, giving no reason for his decision. He was too full of thought, too heavily laden with anxiety to speak much. 'Come, let's get on; you'll want your dinner, and it's getting dark.' So they cantered on, and got off their horses at the gate without another word. And not another word was spoken on the subject that night. Harry was very silent, walking up and down the verandah with his pipe in his mouth—not lying on the ground in idle enjoyment—and there was no reading. The two sisters looked at him from time to time with wistful anxious eyes, half afraid to disturb him by speech.

As for him—he felt that the weight was all on his own shoulders. He had worked hard, and was on the way to be rich. I do not know that he thought much about money, but he thought very much of success; and he was by nature anxious, sanguine, and impulsive. There might be before him, within the next week, such desolation as would break his heart. He knew men who had been ruined and had borne their ruin almost without a wail, who had seemed contented to descend to security and mere absence from want. There was his own superintendent, old Bates, who, though he grumbled at everything else, never bewailed his own fate. But he knew of himself that any such blow would nearly kill him—such a blow, that is, as might drive him from Gangoil, and force him to be the servant instead of the master of men. Not to be master of all around him seemed to him to be misery. The merchants at Brisbane, who took his wool and supplied him with stores, had advanced money when he first bought his run, and he still owed them some thousands of pounds. The injury which a great fire would do him would bring him to such a condition that the merchants would demand to have their money repaid. He understood it all, and knew well that it was after this fashion that many a squatter before him had been ruined.*

'Speak a word to me about it,' his wife said to him imploringly, when they were alone together that night.

'My darling, if there were a word to say, I would say it. I must be on the watch and do the best I can. At present the earth is too damp for mischief.'

'Oh that it would rain again!'

'There will be heat enough before the summer is over; we need not doubt that. But I will tell you of everything as we go on. I will endeavour to have the man watched. God bless you! Go to sleep, and try to get it out of your thoughts.'

On the following morning he breakfasted early and mounted his horse without saying a word as to the purport of his journey. This was in accordance with the habit of his life, and would not excite observation; but there was something in his manner which made both the ladies feel that he was intent on some special object. When he intended simply to ride round his fences or to visit the hut of some distant servant, a few minutes signified nothing. He would stand under the verandah and talk, and the women would endeavour to keep him from the saddle. But now there was no loitering, and but little talking. He said a word to Jacko, who brought the horse for him, and then started at a gallop towards the wool-shed. He did not stop a moment at the shed—not even entering it to see whether the heap of leaves had been displaced during the night—but went on straight to Medlicot's Mill. He rode the nine miles in an hour, and at once entered the building in which the canes were crushed. The first man he met was Nokes, who acted as overseer, having a gang of Polynesian labourers under him, sleek, swarthy fellows, from the South Sea Islands,* with linen trousers on and nothing else, who crept silently among the vats and machinery, shifting the sugar as it was made.

'Well, Nokes,' said Harry, 'how are you getting on? Is Mr Medlicot here?'

Nokes was a big fellow, with a broad, solid face, which would not have condemned him among physiognomists, but for a bad eye, which could not look you in the face. He had been a boundary-rider for Heathcote, and on an occasion had been impertinent, refusing to leave the yard behind the house unless something was done which those about the place refused to do for him. During the discussion Harry had come in. The man had been drinking, and was still insolent, and Harry had ejected him violently, thrusting him over a gate. The man had returned the next morning, and had then been sent about his business. He had been employed at Medlicot's Mill, but from the day of his dismissal to this, he and Harry had never met each other face to face.

'I'm pretty well, thank ye, Mr Heathcote. I hope you're the same, and the ladies. The master's about somewhere, I take it. Picky, go and find the master.' Picky was one of the Polynesians, who at once started on his errand.

'Have you been over to Gangoil since you left it?' said Harry, looking the man full in the face.

'Not I, Mr Heathcote. I never go where I've had words. And, to tell you the truth, sugar is better than sheep. I'm very comfortable here, and I never liked your work.'

'You haven't been at the wool-shed?'

'What, the Gangoil shed? What the blazes 'd I go there for? It's a matter of ten miles from here.'

'Seven, Nokes.'

'Seven, is it? It is a longish seven miles, Mr Heathcote. How could I get that distance? I ain't so good at walking as I was before I was hurt. You should have remembered that, Mr Heathcote, when you laid hands on me the other day.'

'You're not much the worse for what I did, nor yet for the accident, I take it. At any rate, you've not been at Gangoil wool-shed?'

'No, I've not,' said the man roughly. 'What the mischief should I be doing at your shed at night time?'

'I said nothing about night time.'

'I'm here all day, ain't I? If you're going to palm up any story against me, Mr Heathcote, you'll find yourself in the wrong box. What I does, I does on the square.'

Heathcote was now quite sure that Jacko had been right. He had not doubted much before, but now he did not doubt at all but that the man with whom he was speaking was the wretch who was endeavouring to ruin him; and he felt certain, also, that Jacko was true to him. He knew, too, that he had plainly declared his suspicion to the man himself; but he had resolved upon doing this. He could in no way assist himself in circumventing the man's villany by keeping his suspicion to himself. The man might be frightened, and, in spite of all that had passed between him and Medlicot, he still thought it possible that he might induce the sugar-grower to co-operate with him in driving Nokes from the neighbourhood. He had spent the night in thinking over it all, and this was the resolution to which he had come.

'There's the master,' said Nokes. 'If you've got anything to say about anything you'd better say it to him.'

Harry had never before set his foot upon Medlicot's land since it had been bought away from his own run, and had felt that he would almost demean himself by doing so. He had often looked at the canes from over his own fence, as he had done on the night of the rain, but he had stood always on his own land. Now he was in the sugar mill— never before having seen such a building.

'You've a deal of machinery here, Mr Medlicot,' he said.

'It's a small affair after all,' said the other. 'I hope to get a good plant before I've done.'

'Can I speak a word with you?'

'Certainly. Will you come into the office, or will you go across to the house?'

Harry said that the office would do, and followed Medlicot into a little box-like enclosure which contained a desk and two stools.

'Not much of an office, is it? What can I do for you, Mr Heathcote?'

Then Harry began his story, which he told at considerable length. He apologized for troubling his neighbour at all on the subject, and endeavoured to explain, somewhat awkwardly, that as Mr Medlicot was a new comer, he probably might not understand the kind of treatment to which employers in the bush were occasionally subject from their men. On this matter he said much which, had he been a better tactician, he might probably have left unspoken. He then went on to the story of his own quarrel with Nokes, who had, in truth, been grossly impudent to the women about the house, but who had been punished by instant and violent dismissal from his employment. It was evidently Harry's idea that a man who had so sinned against his master should be allowed to find no other master—at any rate in that district—an idea with which the other man, who had lately come out from the old country, did not at all sympathize.

'Do you want me to dismiss him?' said Medlicot, in a tone which implied that that would be the last thing he would think of doing.

'You haven't heard me yet.' Then Harry went on and told of the fires in the heat of summer, and of their terrible effects, of the easy manner of revenge which they supplied to angry, unscrupulous men, and of his own fears at the present moment.

'I can believe it all,' said Medlicot, 'and am very sorry that it should be so. But I cannot see the justice of punishing a man on the merest, vaguest suspicion. Your only ground for imputing this crime to him is that your own conduct to him may have given him a motive.'

Harry had schooled himself vigorously during the ride as to his own demeanour, and had resolved that he would be cool. 'I was going on to tell you,' he said, 'what occurred that night after I saw you up by the fence.'

Then he described how he and his boy had entered the shed and had both seen and heard a man as he escaped from it; how the boy had at once declared that the man was Nokes; how the following day he had discovered the leaves, which Nokes no doubt had deposited there just before the rain, intending to burn the place at once; and how Nokes's manner to him within the last half hour had corroborated his suspicions.

'Is he the boy you call Jacko?'

'That's the name he goes by.'

'You don't know his real name?'

'I have never heard any other name.'

'Nor anything about him?'

Harry owned, in answer to half a dozen such questions, that Jacko had come to Gangoil about four months ago—he did not know whence—had been kept for a week's job, and had then been allowed to remain about the place without any regular wages.

'You admit it was quite dark,' continued Medlicot.

Harry did not at all like the cross-examination, and his resolution to be cool was quickly fading. 'I told you that I saw, myself, the figure of a man.'

'But that you barely saw a figure. You did not form any opinion of your own as to the man's identity.'

Harry Heathcote was as honest as the sun. Much as he disliked being cross-examined, he found himself compelled not only to say the exact truth, but the whole truth. 'Certainly not. I barely saw a glimpse of a figure, and, till I spoke to Nokes just now, I almost doubted whether the lad could have distinguished him. I am sure he was right now.'

'Really, Mr Heathcote, I can't go along with you. You are accusing a man of committing an offence, which I believe is capital, on the evidence of a boy of whom you know nothing, who may have his own reasons for spiting the man, and whom you yourself did not believe till you had looked this man in the face. I think you allow yourself to be guided too much by your own power of intuition.'

'No, I don't,' said Harry, who hated his neighbour's methodical argument.

'At any rate I can't consent to take a man's bread out of his mouth, and to send him away tainted as he would be with this suspicion, either because Jacko thought that he saw him in the dark, or because—'

'I have never asked you to send him away.'

'What is it you want then?'

'I want to have him watched, so that he may feel that, if he attempts to destroy my property, his guilt will be detected.'

'Who is to watch him?'

'He is in your employment.'

'He lives in the hut down beyond the gate. Am I to keep a sentry there all night and every night?'

'I will pay for it.'

'No, Mr Heathcote. I don't pretend to know this country yet, but I'll encourage no such espionage as that. At any rate it is not English. I dare say the man misbehaved himself in your employment. You say he was drunk. I do not doubt it. But he is not a drunkard, for he never drinks here. A man is not to starve for ever because he once got drunk and was impertinent, nor is he to have a spy at his heels because a boy whom nobody knows chooses to denounce him. I am sorry that you should be in trouble, but I do not know that I can help you.'

Harry's passion was now very high, and his resolution to be cool was almost thrown to the winds. Medlicot had said many things which were odious to him. In the first place, there had been a tone of insufferable superiority—so Harry thought—and that, too, when he himself had divested himself of all the superiority which naturally attached to his position, and had frankly appealed to Medlicot as a neighbour. And then this newfangled sugar-grower had told him that he was not English, and had said grand words, and had altogether made himself objectionable. What did this man know of the Australian bush, that he should dare to talk of this or that as being wrong because it was un-English? In England there were police to guard men's property. Here, out in the Australian forests, a man must guard his own or lose it. But perhaps it was the indifference to the ruin of the women belonging to him that Harry Heathcote felt the strongest. The stranger cared nothing for the utter desolation which one unscrupulous ruffian might produce—felt no horror at the idea of a vast devastating fire; but could be indignant in his mock philanthropy because it was proposed to watch the doings of a scoundrel! 'Good morning,' said Harry, turning round and leaving the office brusquely. Medlicot followed him, but Harry went so quickly that not another word was spoken. To him the idea of a neighbour in the bush refusing such assistance as he had asked was as terrible as to us is the thought of a ship at sea leaving another ship in distress. He unhitched his horse from the fence, and galloped home as fast as the animal would carry him.

Medlicot, when he was left alone, took two or three turns about the mill, as though inspecting the work, but at every turn fixed his eyes for a few moments on Nokes's face. The man was standing under a huge caldron, regulating the escape of the boiling juice into the different vats by raising and lowering a trap, and giving directions to the Polynesians as he did so. He was evidently conscious that he was being regarded, and, as is usual in such a condition, manifestly failed in his struggle to appear unconscious. Medlicot acknowledged to himself that the man could not look even him in the face. Was it possible that he had been wrong, and that Heathcote, though he had expressed himself badly, was entitled to some sympathy in his fear of what might be done to him by an enemy? Medlicot also desired to be just, being more rational, more logical, and less impulsive than the other—being also somewhat too conscious of his own superior intelligence. He knew that Heathcote had gone away in great dudgeon, and he almost feared that he had been harsh and unneighbourly. After a while he stood opposite Nokes and addressed him. 'Do the squatters suffer much from fires?' he said.

'Heathcote has been talking to you about that,' said the man.

'Can't you say "Mr Heathcote" when you speak of a gentleman whose bread you have eaten?'

'Mr Heathcote, if you like it. We ain't particular to a shade out here as you are at home. He has been telling you about fires, has he?'

'Well, he has.'

'And talking of me, I suppose?'

'You were talking of having a turn at mining some day. How would it be with you if you were to be off to Gympie?'*

'You mean to say I'm to go, Mr Medlicot?'

'I don't say that at all.'

'Look here, Mr Medlicot. My going or staying won't make any difference to Heathcote. There's a lot of 'em about here hates him that much that he is never to be allowed to rest in peace. I tell you that fairly. It ain't anything as I shall do. Them's not my ways, Mr Medlicot. But he has enemies here as'll never let him rest.'

'Who are they?'

'Pretty nigh everybody round. He has carried himself that high they won't stand him. Who's Heathcote?'

'Name some who are his enemies.'

'There's the Brownbies.'

'Oh, the Brownbies! Well, it's a bad thing to have enemies.' After that he left the sugar-house and went across to the cottage.

CHAPTER V

BOSCOBEL

TWO days and two nights passed without fear of fire, and then Harry Heathcote was again on the alert. The earth was parched as though no drop of rain had fallen; the fences were dry as tinder, and the ground was strewed with broken atoms of timber from the trees, each of which a spark would ignite. Two nights Harry slept in his bed, but on the third he was on horse-back about the run, watching, thinking, endeavouring to make provision, directing others, and hoping to make it believed that his eyes were everywhere. In this way an entire week was passed, and now it wanted but four days to Christmas. He would come home to breakfast about seven in the morning, very tired, but never owning that he was tired, and then sleep heavily for an hour or two in a chair. After that he would go out again on the run, would sleep perhaps for another hour after dinner, and then would start for his night's patrol. During this week he saw nothing of Medlicot, and never mentioned his name but once. On that occasion his wife told him that during his absence Medlicot had been at the station.

'What brought him here?' Harry asked fiercely.

Mrs Heathcote explained that he had called in a friendly way, and had said that if there were any fear of fire he would be happy himself to lend assistance.

Then the young squatter forgot himself in his wrath. 'Confound his hypocrisy!' said Harry, aloud.

'I don't think he's a hypocrite,' said the wife.

'I'm sure he's not,' said Kate Daly.

Not a word more was spoken, and Harry immediately left the house. The two women did not as usual go to the gate to see him mount his horse—not refraining from doing so in any anger, or as wishing to exhibit displeasure at Harry's violence, but because they were afraid of him. They had found themselves compelled to differ from him, but were oppressed at finding themselves in opposition to him.

The feeling that his wife should in any way take part against him added greatly to Heathcote's trouble. It produced in his mind a terrible feeling of loneliness in his sorrow. He bore a brave outside to all his men, and to any stranger whom in these days he met about the run—to his wife and sister also, and to the old woman at home. He forced upon them all an idea that he was not only autocratic but self-sufficient also—that he wanted neither help nor sympathy. He never cried out in his pain, being heartily ashamed even of the appeal which he had made to Medlicot. He spoke aloud and laughed with the men, and never acknowledged that his trials were almost too much for him. But he was painfully conscious of his own weakness. He sometimes felt, when alone in the bush, that he would fain get off his horse and lie upon the ground and weep till he slept. It was not that he trusted no one. He suspected no one with a positive suspicion except Nokes, and Medlicot as the supporter of Nokes. But he had no one with whom he could converse freely, none whom he had not been accustomed to treat as the mere ministers of his will except his wife and his wife's sister, and now he was disjoined from them by their sympathy with Medlicot! He had chosen to manage everything himself, without contradiction and almost without counsel; but, like other such imperious masters, he now found that when trouble came the privilege of dictatorship brought with it an almost insupportable burden.

Old Bates was an excellent man, of whose fidelity the young squatter was quite assured. No one understood footrot better than old Bates, or was less sparing of himself in curing it. He was a second mother to all the lambs, and, when shearing came, watched with the eyes of Argus to see that the sheep were not wounded by the shearers, or the wool left on their backs. But he had no conversation, none of that imagination which in such a time as this might have assisted in devising safeguards, and but little enthusiasm. Shepherds, so-called, Harry kept none upon the run, and would have felt himself insulted had any one suggested that he was so backward in his ways as to employ men of that denomination. He had fenced his run, and dispensed with shepherds and shepherding as old-fashioned and unprofit-able. He had two mounted men, whom he called bound-ary-riders—one an Irishman and the other a German—and them he trusted fully, the German altogether and the Irishman equally as regarded his honesty; but he could not explain to them the thoughts that loaded his brain. He could instigate them to eagerness; but he could not conde-scend to tell Karl Bender, the German, that if his fences were destroyed, neither his means nor his credit would be sufficient to put them up again, and that if the scanty herbage were burnt off any large proportion of his run, he must sell his flocks at a great sacrifice. Nor could he explain to Mickey O'Dowd, the Irishman, that his peace of mind was destroyed by his fear of one man. He had to bear it all alone. And there was heavy on him also the great misery of feeling that everything might depend on his own exer-tions, and that yet he did not know how or where to exert himself. When he had ridden about all night and discovered nothing, he might just as well have been in bed; and he was continually riding about all night and discovering nothing.

After leaving the station on the evening of the day on which he had expressed himself to the women so vehement-ly respecting Medlicot, he met Bates coming home from his day's work. It was then past eight o'clock, and the old man was sitting wearily on his horse, with his head low down between his shoulders, and the reins hardly held within his grasp.

'You're late, Mr Bates,' said Harry; 'you take too much out of yourself this hot weather.'

'I've got to move slower, Mr Heathcote, as I grow older— that's about it—and the beast I'm on is not much good.'

Now Mr Bates was always complaining of his horse, and yet was allowed to choose any on the run for his own use.

'If you don't like him, why don't you take another?'

'There ain't much difference in 'em, Mr Heathcote. Better the devil you know than the devil you don't. It's getting uncommon close shaving for them wethers in the new paddock. They're down upon the roots pretty well already.'

'There's grass along the bush on the north side.'

'They won't go there; it's rank and sour. They won't feed up there as long as they can live lower down and nearer the water. Weather like this, they'd sooner die near the water than travel to fill their bellies. It's about the hottest day we've had, and the nights a'most hotter. Are you going to be out, Mr Heathcote?'

'I think so.'

'What's the good of it, Mr Heathcote? There is no use in it. Lord love you! what can you do? You can't be every side at once.'

'Fire can only travel with the wind, Mr Bates.'

'And there isn't any wind, and so there can't be any fire. I never did think, and I don't think now, there ever was any use in a man fashing himself as you fash yourself. You can't alter things, Mr Heathcote.'

'But that's just what I can do—what a man has to do. If a match were thrown there, at your feet, and the grass was aflame, couldn't you alter that by putting your foot on it? If you find a ewe on her back, can't you alter that by putting her on her legs?'

'Yes, I can do that, I suppose.'

'What does a man live for except to alter things? When a man clears the forest, and sows corn, does he not alter things?'

'That's not your line, Mr Heathcote,' said the cunning old man.

'If I send wool to market, I alter things.'

'You'll excuse me, Mr Heathcote. Of course I'm old, but I just give you my experience.'

'I'm much obliged to you, though we can't always agree, you know. Good night. Go in and say a word to my wife, and tell them you saw me all right.'

'I'll have a crack with 'em, Mr Heathcote, before I turn in.'

'And tell Mary I sent my love.'

'I will, Mr Heathcote, I will.'

He was thinking always of his wife during his solitary rides, and of her fear and deep anxiety. It was for her sake and for the children that he was so careworn—not for his own. Had he been alone in the world he would not have fretted himself in this fashion because of the malice of any man. But how would it be with her, should he be forced to move her from Gangoil? And yet, with all his love, they had parted almost in anger. Surely she would understand the tenderness of the message he had just sent her?

Of a sudden, as he was riding, he stopped his horse and listened attentively. From a great distance there fell upon his accustomed ear a sound which he recognized, though he was aware that the place from whence it came was at least two miles distant. It was the thud of an axe against a tree. He listened still, and was sure that it was so, and turned at once toward the sound, though in doing so he left his course at a right angle. He had been going directly away from the river, with his back to the wool-shed; but now he changed his course, riding in the direction of the spot at which Jacko had nearly fallen in jumping over the fence. As he continued on, the sounds became plainer, till at last, reining in his horse, he could see the form of the woodman, who was still at work ringing the trees. This was a job which the man did by contract, receiving so much an acre for the depopulation of the timber. It was now bright moonlight, almost as clear as day—a very different night indeed from that on which the rain had come—and Harry could see at a glance that it was the man called Boscobel, still at work. Now there were, as he thought, very good reasons why Boscobel at the present moment should not be so employed. Boscobel was receiving wages for work of another kind.

'Bos,' said the squatter, riding up, and addressing the man by the customary abbreviation of his nickname, 'I thought you were watching at Brownbie's boundary?' Boscobel lowered his axe, and stood for a while contemplating the proposition made to him. 'You are drawing three shillings a night for watching; isn't that so?'

'Yes, that's so. Anyways, I shall draw it.'

'Then why ain't you watching?'

'There's nothing to watch that I knows on—not just now.'

'Then why should I pay you for it? I'm to pay you for ringing these trees, ain't I?'

'Certainly, Mr Heathcote.'

'Then you're to make double use of your time, and sell it twice over, are you? Don't try to look like a fool, as though you didn't understand. You know that what you're doing isn't honest.'

'Nobody ever said as I wasn't honest before.'

'I tell you so now. You're robbing me of the time you've sold to me, and for which I'm to pay you.'

'There ain't nothing to watch while the wind's as it is now, and that chap ain't anywhere about to-night.'

'What chap?'

'Oh, I know. I'm all right. What's the use of dawdling about up there in the broad moonlight, and the wind like this?'

'That's for me to judge. If you engage to do my work and take my money, you're swindling me when you go about another job, as you are now. You needn't scratch your head. You understand it all as well as I do.'

'I never was told I swindled before, and I ain't a-going to put up with it. You may ring your own trees, and watch your own fences, and the whole place may be burned for me. I ain't a-going to do another turn in Gangoil. Swindle, indeed!' So Boscobel shouldered his axe and marched off through the forest, visible in the moonlight till the trees hid him.

There was another enemy made! He had never felt quite sure of this man, but had been glad to have him about the place as being thoroughly efficient in his own business. It was only during the last ten days that he had agreed to pay him for night watching, leaving the man to do as much additional day-work as he pleased, for which, of course, he would be paid at the regular contract price. There was a double purpose intended in this watching, as was well understood by all the hands employed; first, that of preventing incendiary fire by the mere presence of the watchers, and, secondly, that of being at hand to extinguish fire in case of need. Now a man ringing trees five or six miles away from the beat on which he was stationed could not serve either of these purposes. Boscobel, therefore, had been fraudulently at work for his own dishonest purposes, and knew well that his employment was of that nature. All this was quite clear to Heathcote; and it was clear to him also that when he detected fraud he was bound to expose it. Had the man acknowledged his fault, and been submissive, there would have been an end of the matter. Heathcote would have said no word about it to any one, and would not have stopped a farthing from the week's unearned wages. That he had to encounter a certain amount of ill-usage from the rough men about him, and to forgive it, he could understand; but it could not be his duty either as a man or a master to pass over dishonesty without noticing it. No; that he would not do, though Gangoil should burn from end to end. He did not much mind being robbed. He knew that to a certain extent he must endure to be

cheated—he would endure it—but he would never teach
his men to think that he passed over such matters because
he was afraid of them, or that dishonesty on their part was
indifferent to him.

But now he had made another enemy—an enemy of a
man who had declared to him that he knew the movements
of 'that chap,' meaning Nokes! How hard the world was!
It seemed that all around were trouble to him. He turned
his horse back, and made again for the spot which was his
original destination. As he cantered on among the trees,
twisting here and there, and regulating his way by the stars,
he asked himself whether it would not be better for him to
go home and lay himself down by his wife and sleep, and
await the worst that these men could do to him. This idea
was so strong upon him that at one spot he made his horse
stop till he had thought it all out. No one encouraged him
in his work. Every one about the place, friend or foe, Bates,
his wife, Medlicot, and this Boscobel spoke to him as
though he were fussy and fidgety in his anxiety. 'If fires
must come, they will come; and if they are not to come,
you are simply losing your labour.' This was the upshot of
all they said to him. Why should he be wiser than they? If
the ruin came, let it come. Old Bates had been ruined, but
still had enough to eat and drink, and clothes to wear, and
did not work half as hard as his employer. He thought that
if he could only find some one person who would sympathize with him, and support him, he would not mind; but the
mental loneliness of his position almost broke his heart.

Then there came across his mind the dim remembrance
of certain old school-words,* and he touched his horse with
his spur and hurried onwards. Let there be no steps backward. A thought as to the manliness of persevering, of the
want of manliness in yielding to depression, came to his
rescue. Let him at any rate have the comfort of thinking
that he had done his best according to his lights. After some
dim fashion, he did come to recognize it as a fact that

nothing could really support him but self-approbation. Though he fell from his horse in utter weariness, he would persevere.

As the night wore on he came to the German's hut, and, finding it empty, as he expected, rode on to the outside fence of his run. When he reached this he got off his horse, and, taking a key out of his pocket, whistled upon it loudly. A few minutes afterwards the German came up to him.

'There's been no one about, I suppose?' he asked.

'Not a one,' said the man.

'You've been across on Brownbie's run?'

'Ve're on it now, Mr 'Eathcote.' They were both on the side of the fence away from Gangoil station.

'I don't know how that is, Karl. I think Gangoil goes a quarter of a mile beyond this. But we did not quite strike the boundary when we put up the fence.'

'Brownbie's cattle is allays here, Mr 'Eathcote, and is knocking down the fence every day. Brownbie is a rascal, and 'is cattle as bad as 'isself.'

'Never mind that, Karl, now. When we've got through the heats, we'll put a mile or two of better fencing along here. You know Boscobel?'

'In course I know Bos.'

'What sort of a fellow is he?' Then Harry told his German dependent exactly what had taken place between him and the other man.

'He's in and in wid all them young Brownbies,' said Karl.

'The Brownbies are a bad lot, but I don't think they'd do anything of this kind,' said Harry, whose mind was still dwelling on the dangers of fire.

'They likes muttons, Mr 'Eathcote.'

'I suppose they do take a sheep or two now and then. They wouldn't do worse than that, would they?'

'Noting too 'ot for 'em; noting too 'eavy,' said Karl, smoking his pipe. 'The vind, vat there is, comes just here,

Mr 'Eathcote,' and the man lifted up his arm and pointed across in the direction of Brownbie's run.

'And you don't think much of Boscobel?' Karl Bender shook his head. 'He was always well treated here,' said Harry, 'and has had plenty of work, and earned large wages. The man will be a fool to quarrel with me.' Karl again shook his head. With Karl Bender Harry was quite sure of his man, but not on that account need he be quite sure of the correctness of the man's opinion.

Thence he went on till he met his other lieutenant, O'Dowd; and so, having completed his work, he made his way home, reaching the station at sunrise.

'Did Bates tell you he'd met me?' he asked his wife.

'Yes, Harry; kiss me, Harry! I was so glad you sent a word. Promise me, Harry, not to think that I don't agree with you in everything.'

CHAPTER VI

THE BROWNBIES OF BOOLABONG*

OLD BROWNBIE, as he was usually called, was a squatter also, but a squatter of a class very different from that to which Heathcote belonged. He had begun his life in the colonies a little under a cloud, having been sent out from home after the perpetration of some peccadillo of which the law had disapproved. In colonial phrase, he was a 'lag,' having been transported; but this was many years ago, when he was quite young, and he had now been a free man for more than thirty years.* It must be owned on his behalf that he had worked hard, had endeavoured to rise, and had risen; but there still stuck to him the savour of his old life. Every one knew that he had been a convict; and even had he become a man of high principle—a condition which he certainly never achieved—he could hardly have escaped altogether from the thraldom of his degradation. He had been a butcher, a drover, part owner of stock, and had at last become possessed of a share of a cattle run, and then of the entire property, such as it was. He had four or five sons, uneducated, ill-conditioned, drunken fellows, who had all their father's faults without his energy, some of whom had been in prison, and all of whom were known as pests to the colony. Their place was called Boolabong, and was a cattle run, as distinguished from a sheep run; but it was a poor place, was sometimes altogether unstocked, and was supposed to be not unfrequently used as a receptacle for stolen cattle. The tricks which the Brownbies played with cattle were notorious throughout Queensland and New South Wales, and by a certain class of men were much admired. They would drive a few head of cattle—perhaps forty or fifty—for miles around the country, across one station and another, travelling many hundreds of miles, and here and there as they passed along they would sweep into their own herd the bullocks of the victims whose lands they passed. If detected on the spot, they gave up their prey. They were in the right in moving their own cattle, and were not responsible for the erratic tendencies of other animals. If successful, they either sold their stolen beasts to butchers on the road, or got them home to Boolabong. There were dangers, of course, and occasional penalties; but there was much success. It was supposed also that, though they did not own sheep, they preferred mutton for their daily uses, and that they supplied themselves at a very cheap rate. It may be imagined how such a family would be hated by the respectable squatters on whom they preyed. Still there were men—old stagers, who had known Moreton Bay before it was a colony,* in the old days when convicts were common—who almost regarded the Brownbies as a part of the common order of things, and who were indisposed to persecute them. Men must live, and what were a few sheep? Of some such it might be said that, though they were above the arts by which the Brownbies lived, they were not very scrupulous themselves, and it perhaps served them to have within their ken neighbours whose morality was lower even than their own. But to such a one as Harry Heathcote the Brownbies were utterly abominable. He was for law and justice at any cost. To his thinking the Colonial Government was grossly at fault because it did not weed out and extirpate, not only the identical Brownbies, but all Brownbieism wherever it might be found. A dishonest workman was a great evil, but to his thinking a dishonest man in the position of master was the incarnation of evil. As to difficulties of evidence, and obstacles of that nature, Harry Heathcote knew nothing. The Brownbies were rascals, and should therefore be exterminated.

And the Brownbies knew well the estimation in which their neighbour held them. Harry had made himself altogether disagreeable to them. They were squatters as well as he, or at least so they termed themselves; and though they would not have expected to be admitted to home intimacies, they thought that when they were met out of doors, or in public places, they should be treated with some respect. On such occasions Harry treated them as though they were dirt beneath his feet. The Brownbies would be found, whenever a little money came among them, at the public billiard-rooms and race-courses within 150 miles of Boolabong.* At such places Harry Heathcote was never seen. It would have been as easy to seduce the Bishop of Brisbane into a bet as Harry Heathcote. He had never even drank a nobbler with one of the Brownbies. To their thinking he was a proud, stuck-up, unsocial young cub, whom to rob was a pleasure, and to ruin would be a delight.

The old man at Boolabong was now almost obsolete. Property that he could keep in his grasp there was in truth none. He was the tenant of the run under the Crown, and his sons could not turn him out of the house. The cattle, when there were cattle, belonged to them. They were in no respect subject to his orders, and he would have had a bad life among them were it not that they quarrelled among themselves, and that in such quarrels he could belong to one party or to the other. The house itself was a wretched place, out of order, with doors and windows and floors shattered, broken, and decayed. There were none of womankind belonging to the family, and in such a house a decent woman-servant would have been out of her place. Sometimes there was one hag there, and sometimes another, and sometimes feminine aid less respectable than that of the hags. There had been six sons. One had disappeared utterly, so that nothing was known of him. One had been absolutely expelled by the brethren, and was now a vagabond in the country, turning up now and then at Boolabong and demanding food. Of the whole lot, Georgie Brownbie, the vagabond, was the worst. The eldest son was at this time in prison at Brisbane, having on some late occasion been less successful than usual in regard to some acquired bullocks. The three youngest were at home—Jerry, Jack, and Joe. Tom, who was in prison, was the only staunch friend to the father, who consequently at this time was in a more than usually depressed condition.

Christmas Day would fall on a Tuesday, and on the Sunday before it* Jerry Brownbie, the eldest of those now at home, was sitting with a pipe in his mouth on a broken-down stool on the broken-down verandah of the house, and the old man was seated on a stuffy, worn-out sofa with three legs, which was propped against the wall of the house and had not been moved for years. Old Brownbie was a man of gigantic frame, and had possessed immense personal power; a man, too, of will and energy, but he was now worn out and dropsical, and could not move beyond the confines of the home station. The verandah was attached to a big room which ran nearly the whole length of the house, and which was now used for all purposes. There was an exterior kitchen, in which certain processes were carried on, such as salting stolen mutton and boiling huge masses of meat, when such work was needed. But the cookery was generally done in the big room. And here also two or three of the sons slept on beds made upon stretchers along the wall. They were not probably very particular as to which owned each bed, enjoying a fraternal communism in that respect. At the end of this chamber the old man had a room of his own. Boolabong was certainly a miserable place; and yet, such as it was, it was frequented by many guests. The vagabondism of the colonies is proverbial. Vagabonds are taken in almost everywhere throughout the bush;* but the welcome given to them varies. Sometimes they are made to work before they are fed, to their infinite disgust; but no such cruelty was exercised at Boolabong. Boolabong was a very paradise for vagabonds. There was always flour and meat to be had, generally tobacco, and

sometimes even the luxury of a nobbler. The Brownbies
were wise enough to have learned that it was necessary for
their very existence that they should have friends in the
land. On the Sunday the father and Jerry Brownbie were
sitting out in the verandah at about noon, and the other
two sons, Jack and Joe, were lying asleep on the beds
within.

The heat of the day was intense. There was a wind
blowing, but it was that which is called there the hot wind,
which comes dry, scorching, sometimes almost intolerable,
over the burning central plain of the country. No one can
understand without feeling it how much a wind can add to
the sufferings inflicted by heat. The old man had on a dirty,
wretched remnant of a dressing-gown, but Jerry was clothed
simply in trousers and an old shirt. Only that the musquitoes would have flayed him he would have dispensed
probably with these. He had been quarrelling with his
father respecting a certain horse which he had sold, of the
price of which the father demanded a share. Jerry had
unblushingly declared that he himself had 'shaken' the
horse* (Anglice, had stolen him twelve months since on
Darling Downs),* and was therefore clearly entitled to the
entire plunder. The father had rejoined with animation that
unless 'half a quid'—or 10s.—were given him as his con-
tribution to the keep of the animal, he would inform against
his son to the squatter on the Darling Downs,* and had
shown him that he knew the very run from which the horse
had been taken. Then the sons within had interfered from
their beds, swearing that their father was the noisiest old
'cuss' unhung—they having had their necessary slumbers
disturbed.

At this moment the debate was interrupted by the appearance of a man outside the verandah.

'Well, Mr Jerry, how goes it?' asked the stranger.

'What, Bos, is that you? What brings you up to Boolabong? I thought you was ringing trees for that young scut

at Gangoil? I'll be even with him some of these days. He
had the impudence to send a man of his up here last week
looking for sheepskins!'

'He wasn't that soft, Mr Jerry, was he? Well, I've dropped
working for him. How are you, Mr Brownbie? I hope I see
you finely, sir. It's stiffish sort of weather, Mr Brownbie,
ain't it, sir?'

The old man grunted out some reply, and then asked
Boscobel what he wanted.

'I'll just hang about for the day, Mr Brownbie, and get
a little grub. You never begrudged a working man that yet.'

Old Brownbie again grunted, but said no word of welcome. That, however, was to be taken for granted, without
much expression of opinion.

'No, Mr Jerry,' continued Boscobel, 'I've done with that
fellow.'

'And so has Nokes done with him.'

'Nokes is at work on Medlicot's Mill. That sugar business
wouldn't suit me.'

'An axe in your hand is what you're fit for, Bos.'

'There's a many things I can turn my hand to, Mr Jerry.
You couldn't give a fellow such a thing as a nobbler, Mr
Jerry, could you? I'd offer money for it, only I know it
would be taken amiss. It's that hot that a fellow's very
in'ards get parched up.'

Upon this Jerry slowly rose, and, going to a cupboard,
brought forth a modicum of spirits, which he called 'Battle
Axe,' but which was supposed to be brandy. This Boscobel
swallowed at a gulp, and then washed it down with a little
water.

'Come, Jerry,' said the old man, somewhat relenting in his
wrath, 'you might as well give us a drop as it's going about.'

The two brothers, who had now been thoroughly aroused
from their sleep, and who had heard the enticing sound of
the spirit bottle, joined the party, and so they drank all
round.

'Heathcote's in an awful state about them fires, ain't he?' asked Jerry.

Boscobel, who had squatted down on the verandah, and was now lighting his pipe, bobbed his head.

'I wish he was clean burned out—over head and ears,' said Jerry.

Boscobel bobbed his head again, sucking with great energy at the closely-stuffed pipe.

'If he treated me like he does you fellows,' continued Jerry, 'he shouldn't have a yard of fencing or a blade of grass left, nor a ewe, nor a lamb, nor a hogget. I do hate fellows who come here and want to be better than any one about 'em—young chaps especially. Sending up here to look for sheepskins, cuss his impudence! I sent that German fellow of his away with a flea in his ear.'

'Karl Bender?'

'It's some such name as that.'

'He's all in all with the young squire,' said Boscobel. 'And there's a chap there called Jacko—he's another. He gets 'em down there to Gangoil, and the ladies talks to 'em, and then they'd go through fire and water for him. There's Mickey—he's another, just the same way. I don't like them ways myself.'

'Too much of master and man about it; ain't there, Bos?'

'Just that, Mr Jerry. That ain't my idea of a free country. I can work as well as another, but I ain't going to be told that I'm a swindler because I'm making the most of my time.'

'He turned Nokes out by the scruff of his neck?' said Jerry. Boscobel again bobbed his head. 'I didn't think Nokes was the sort of fellow to stand that.'

'No more he ain't,' said Boscobel.

'Heathcote's a good plucked 'un all the same,' said Joe.

'It's like you to speak up for such a fellow as that,' said Jerry.

'I say he's a good plucked 'un. I'm not standing up for him. Nokes is half a stone heavier than him, and ought to have knocked him over. That's what you'd've done; wouldn't you, Bos? I know I would.'

'He'd've had my axe at his head,' said Boscobel.

'We all know Joe's game to the backbone,' said Jerry.

'I'm game enough for you, any way,' said the brother; 'and you can try it out any time you like.'

'That's right; fight like dogs; do,' said the old man.

The quarrel at this point was interrupted by the arrival of another man, who crept up round the corner on to the verandah exactly as Boscobel had done. This was Nokes, of whom they had that moment been speaking. There was silence for a few moments among them, as though they feared that he might have heard them, and Nokes stood hanging his head as though half ashamed of himself. Then they gave him the same kind of greeting as the other men had received. Nobody told him that he was welcome, but the spirit jar was again brought into use, Jerry measuring out the liquor, and it was understood that Nokes was to stay there and get his food. He, too, gave some account of himself, which was supposed to suffice, but which they all knew to be false. It was Sunday, and they were off work at the sugar-mill. He had come across Gangoil run intending to take back with him things of his own which he had left at Bender's hut, and, having come so far, had thought that he would come on and get his dinner at Boolabong. As this was being told a good deal was said of Harry Heathcote. Nokes declared that he had come right across Gangoil, and explained that he would not have been at all sorry to meet Master Heathcote in the bush. Master Heathcote had had his own way up at the station when he was backed by a lot of his own hands; but a good time was coming perhaps. Then Nokes gave it to be understood very plainly that it was the settled purpose of his life to give Harry Heathcote a thrashing. During all this there was an immense amount of bad language, and a large practice of the art which in the colony is called 'blowing.'* Jerry,

Boscobel, and Nokes all boasted, each that on the first occasion he would give Harry Heathcote such a beating that a whole bone should hardly be left in the man's skin.

'There isn't one of you man enough to touch him!' said Joe, who was known as the freest fighter of the Brownbie family.

'And you'd eat him, I suppose?' said Jerry.

'He's not likely to come in my way,' said Joe; 'but if he does, he'll get as good as he brings—that's all.'

This was unpleasant to the visitors, who, of course, felt themselves to be snubbed. Boscobel affected to hear the slight put upon his courage with good humour, but Nokes laid himself down in a corner and sulked. They were soon all asleep, and remained dozing, snoring, changing their uncomfortable positions, and cursing the musquitoes, till about four in the afternoon, when Boscobel got up, shook himself, and made some observation about 'grub.' The meal of the day was then prepared. A certain quantity of flour and raw meat, ample for their immediate wants, was given to the two strangers, with which they retired into the outer kitchen, prepared it for themselves, and there ate their dinner, and each of the brothers did the same for himself in the big room—Joe, the fighting brother, providing for his father's wants as well as his own. One of them had half a leg of cold mutton, so that he was saved the trouble of cooking, but he did not offer to share this comfort with the others. An enormous kettle of tea was made, and that was common among them. While this was being consumed, Boscobel put his head into the room, and suggested that he and his mate wanted a drink; whereupon Jerry, without a word, pointed to the kettle, and Boscobel was allowed to fill two pannikins. Such was the welcome which was always accorded to strangers at Boolabong.

After their meal the men came back on to the verandah, and there was more smoking and sleeping, more boasting and snarling. Different allusions were made to the spirit jar, especially by the old man; but they were made in vain. The 'Battle Axe' was Jerry's own property, and he felt that he had already been almost foolishly liberal. But he had an object in view. He was quite sure that Boscobel and Nokes had not come to Boolabong on the same Sunday by any chance coincidence. The men had something to propose, and in their own way they would make the proposition before they left, and would make it probably to him. Boscobel intended to sleep at Boolabong, but Nokes had explained that it was his purpose to return that night to Medlicot's Mill. The proposition no doubt would be made soon—a little after seven, when the day was preparing to give way suddenly to night. Nokes first walked off, sloping out from the verandah in a half shy, half cunning manner, looking no whither, and saying a word to no one. Quickly after him, Boscobel jumped up suddenly, hitched up his trousers, and followed the first man. At about a similar interval, Jerry passed out through the big room to the yard at the back, and from the yard to a shed that was used as a shambles. Here he found the other two men, and no doubt the proposition was made.

'There's something up,' said the old man as soon as Jerry was gone.

'Of course there's something up,' said Joe. 'Those fellows didn't come all the way to Boolabong for nothing.'

'It's something about young Heathcote,' suggested the father.

'If it is,' said Jack, 'what's that to you?'

'They'll get themselves hanged, that's all about it.'

'That be blowed!' said Jack. 'You go easy and hold your tongue. If you know nothing nobody can hurt you.'

'I know nothing,' said Joe, 'and don't mean. If I had scores to quit with a fellow like Harry Heathcote I should do it after my own fashion. I shouldn't get Boscobel to help me, nor yet such a fellow as Nokes. But it's no business of

mine. Heathcote's made the place too hot to hold him—
that's all about it.'

There was no more said, and in an hour's time Jerry
returned to the family. Neither the father nor brother asked
him any questions, nor did he volunteer any information.

Boolabong was about fourteen miles from Medlicot's Mill.
Nokes had walked this distance in the morning, and now
retraced it at night; not going right across Gangoil, as he
had falsely boasted of doing early in the day, but skirting
it, and keeping on the outside of the fence nearly the whole
distance. At about two in the morning he reached his
cottage outside the mill on the river bank; but he was
unable to skulk in unheard. Some dogs made a noise, and
presently he heard a voice calling him from the house.

'Is that you, Nokes, at this time of night?' asked Mr
Medlicot.

Nokes grunted out some reply, intending to avoid any
further question. But his master came up to the hut door
and asked him where he had been.

'Just amusing myself,' said Nokes.

'It's very late.'

'It's not later for me than for you, Mr Medlicot.'

'That's true. I've just ridden home from Gangoil.'

'From Gangoil? I didn't know you was so friendly there,
Mr Medlicot.'

'And where have you been?'

'Not to Gangoil, anyway. Good night, Mr Medlicot!'

Then the man took himself into his hut, and was safe
from further questioning that night.

CHAPTER VII

'I WISH YOU'D LIKE ME'

ALL the Saturday night Heathcote had been on the run,
and he did not return home to bed till nearly dawn on the
Sunday morning. At about noon, prayers were read out on
the verandah, the congregation consisting of Mrs Heathcote
and her sister, Mrs Growler, and Jacko. Harry himself was
rather averse to this performance, intimating that Mrs
Growler, if she were so minded, could read the prayers for
herself in the kitchen, and that, as regarded Jacko, they
would be altogether thrown away. But his wife had made
a point of maintaining the practice, and he had of course
yielded. The service was not long, and when it was over
Harry got into a chair and was soon asleep. He had been
in the saddle during sixteen hours of the previous day and
night, and was entitled to be fatigued. His wife sat beside
him, every now and again protecting him from the flies,
while Kate Daly sat by with her Bible in her hand.* But
she too, from time to time, was watching her brother-in-law.
The trouble of his spirits and the work that he felt himself
bound to do touched them with a strong feeling, and taught
them to regard him for the time as a young hero.

'How quietly he sleeps!' Kate said. 'The fatigue of the
last week must have been terrible.'

'He is quite, quite knocked up,' said the wife.

'I ain't knocked up a bit,' said Harry, jumping up from his
chair. 'What should knock me up? I wasn't asleep, was I?'

'Just dozing, dear.'

'Ah, well! there isn't anything to do, and it's too hot to
get out. I wonder old Bates didn't come in for prayers.'

'I don't think he cares much for prayers,' said Mrs
Heathcote.

'But he likes an excuse for a nobbler as well as any one. Did I tell you that they had fires over at Jackson's yesterday—at Coolaroo?'

'Was there any harm done?'

'A deal of grass burned, and they had to drive the sheep, which won't serve them this kind of weather. I don't know which I fear most—the grass, the fences, or the sheep. As for the buildings, I don't think they'll try that again.'

'Why not, Harry?'

'The risk of being seen is so great. I can hardly understand that a man like Nokes should have been such a fool as he was.'

'You think it was Nokes?'

'Oh, yes, certainly. In the first place, Jacko is as true as steel. I don't mean to swear by the boy, though I think he is a good boy; but I'm sure he's true in this. And then the man's manner to myself was conclusive. I cannot understand a man in Medlicot's position supporting a fellow like that. By heavens! it nearly drives me mad to think of it. Thousands and thousands of pounds are at stake. All that a man has in the world is exposed to the malice of a scoundrel like Nokes! And then a man who calls himself a gentleman will talk about it being un-English to look after him. He's a "new chum;"* I suppose that's his excuse.'

'If it's a sufficient excuse, you should excuse him,' said Kate, with good feminine logic.

'That's just like you all over. He's good-looking, and therefore it's all right. He ought to have learned better. He ought, at any rate, to believe that men who have been here much longer than he has must know the ways of the country a great deal better.'

'It's Christmas time, Harry,' said his wife, 'and you should endeavour to forgive your neighbours.'

'What sort of a Christmas will it be if you and I, and these young fellows here, and Kate, are all burned out of Gangoil? Here's Bates! Well, Mr Bates, how goes it?'

'Tremendous hot, sir.'

'We've found that out already. You haven't heard where that fellow Boscobel has gone?'

'No, I haven't heard; but he'll be over with some of those Brownbie lads. They say Georgie Brownbie's about the country somewhere. If so, there'll be a row among 'em.'

'When thieves fall out, Mr Bates, honest men come by their own.'

'So they say, Mr Heathcote. All the same, I shouldn't care how far Georgie was away from any place I had to do with.'

Then the young master and his old superintendent sauntered out to his back premises to talk about sheep and fires, and plans for putting out fires. And no doubt Mr Bates had the glass of brandy and water, which he had come to regard as one of his Sunday luxuries. From the back premises they went down to the creek to gauge the water. Then they sauntered on, keeping always in the shade, sitting down here to smoke, and standing up there to discuss the pedigree of some particular ram, till it was past six.

'You may as well come in and dine with us, Mr Bates,' Harry suggested, as they returned towards the station.

Mr Bates said that he thought that he would.

As the same invitation was given on almost every Sunday throughout the year, and was invariably answered in the same way, there was not much excitement in this. But Mr Bates would not have dreamed of going into dinner without being asked.

'That's Medlicot's trap,' said Mr Bates, as they entered the yard. 'I heard wheels when we were in the horse-paddock.'

Harry looked at the trap, and then went quickly into the house. He walked with a rapid step on to the verandah, and there he found the sugar-grower and his mother. Mrs Heathcote looked at her husband almost timidly. She knew from the very sound of his feet that he was perturbed in

spirit. Under his own roof-tree he would certainly be courteous; but there is a constrained courtesy very hard to be
borne, of which she knew him to be capable. He first went
up to the old lady, and to her his greeting was pleasant
enough. Harry Heathcote, though he had assumed the
bush mode of dressing, still retained the manners of a
high-bred gentleman in his intercourse with women. Then,
turning sharply round, he gave his hand to Mr Medlicot.
'I am glad to see you at Gangoil,' he said. 'I was not
fortunate enough to be at home when you called the other
day. Mrs Medlicot must have found the drive very hot, I
fear.'

His wife was still looking into his face, and was reading
there, as in a book, the mingled pride and disdain with
which her husband was exercising civility to his enemy.
Harry's countenance wore a look not difficult of perusal;
and Medlicot could read the lines almost as distinctly as
Harry's wife.

'I have asked Mrs Medlicot to stay and dine with us,'
she said, 'so that she may have it cool for the drive back.'

'I am almost afraid of the bush at night,' said the old
woman.

'You'll have a full moon,' said Harry. 'It will be as light
as day.'

So that was settled. Heathcote thought it odd that the
man whom he regarded as his enemy, whom he had left
at their last meeting in positive hostility, should consent to
accept a dinner under his roof; but that was Medlicot's
affair, not his. They dined at seven, and after dinner strolled
out into the horse-paddock, and down to the creek. As they
started the three men went first, and the ladies followed
them; but Bates soon dropped behind. It was his rest day,
and he had already moved quite as much as was usual with
him on a Sunday.

'I think I was a little hard with you the other day,' said
Medlicot, when they were alone together.

'I suppose we hardly understand each other's ideas,' said Harry. He spoke with a constrained voice and with an almost savage manner, engendered by a determination to hold his own. He would forgive any offence for which an apology was made, but no apology had been made as yet; and, to tell the truth, he was a little afraid that, if they got into an argument on the matter, Medlicot would have the best of it. And there was, too, almost a claim to superiority in Medlicot's use of the word 'hard.' When one man says that he has been hard to another he almost boasts that, on that occasion, he got the better of him.

'That's just it,' said Medlicot; 'we do not quite understand each other. But we might believe in each other all the same, and then the understanding would come. But it isn't just that which I want to say; such talking rarely does any good.'

'What is it, then?'

'You may perhaps be right about that man Nokes.'

'No doubt I may. I know I'm right. When I asked him whether he had been at my shed, what made him say that he hadn't been there at night time? I said nothing about night time. But the man was there at night time, or he wouldn't have used the word.'

'I'm not sure that that is evidence.'

'Perhaps not in England, Mr Medlicot, but it's good enough evidence for the bush. And what made him pretend he didn't know the distances? And why can't he look a man in the face? And why should the boy have said it was he if it wasn't? Of course, if you think well of him, you're right to keep him. But you may take it as a rule out here that when a man has been dismissed it hasn't been done for nothing. Men treated that way should travel out of the country. It's better for all parties. It isn't here as it is at home, where people live so thick together that nothing is thought of a man being dismissed. I was obliged to discharge him, and now he's my enemy.'

'A man may be your enemy without being a felon.'

'Of course he may. I'm his enemy in a way, but I wouldn't hurt a hair of his head unjustly. When I see the attempts made to burn me out, of course I know that an enemy has been at work.'

'Is there no one else has got a grudge against you?'

Harry was silent for a moment. What right had this man to cross-examine him about his enmities—the man whose own position in the place had been one of hostility to him, whom he had almost suspected of harbouring Nokes at the mill simply because Nokes had been dismissed from Gangoil? That suspicion was indeed fading away. There was something in Medlicot's voice and manner which made it impossible to attribute such motives to him. Nevertheless, the man was a free-selector, and had taken a bit of the Gangoil run after a fashion which to Heathcote was objectionable politically, morally, and socially. Let Medlicot in regard to character be what he might, he was a free-selector and a squatter's enemy, and had clinched his hostility by employing a servant dismissed from the very run out of which he had bought his land.

'It is hard to say,' he replied at length, 'who have grudges—or against whom—or why. I suppose I have a grudge against you, if the truth is to be known; but I shan't burn down your mill.'

'I'm sure you won't.'

'Nor yet say worse of you behind your back than I will to your face.'

'I don't want you to think that you have occasion to speak ill of me either one way or the other. What I mean is this—I don't quite think that the evidence against Nokes is strong enough to justify me in sending him away; but I'll keep an eye on him as well as I can. It seems that he left our place early this morning; but the men are not supposed to be there on Sundays, and of course he does as he pleases with himself.'

The conversation then dropped, and in a little time Harry made some excuse for leaving them, and returned to the house alone, promising, however, that he would not start for his night's ride till after the party had come back to the station.

'There is no hurry at all,' he said; 'I shan't stir for two hours yet, but Mickey will be waiting there for stores for himself and the German.'

'That means a nobbler for Mickey,' said Kate. 'Either of those men would think it a treat to ride ten miles in and ten miles back, with a horse-load of sugar and tea and flour, for the sake of a glass of brandy and water.'

'And so would you,' said Harry, 'if you lived in a hut by yourself for a fortnight, with nothing to drink but tea without milk.'

The old lady and Mrs Heathcote were soon seated on the grass, while Medlicot and Kate Daly roamed on together. Kate was a pretty, modest girl, timid withal and shy, unused to society, and therefore awkward, but with the natural instincts and aptitudes of her sex. What the glass of brandy and water was to Mickey O'Dowd after a fortnight's solitude in a bush-hut, with tea, dampers, and lumps of mutton, a young man in the guise of a gentleman was to poor Kate Daly. A brother-in-law, let him be ever so good, is, after all, no better than tea without milk. No doubt Mickey O'Dowd often thought about a nobbler in his thirsty solitude, and so did Kate speculate on what might possibly be the attractions of a lover. Medlicot probably indulged in no such speculations; but the nobbler, when brought close to his lips, was grateful to him as to others. That Kate Daly was very pretty no man could doubt.

'Isn't it sad that he should have to ride about all night like that?' said Kate, to whom, as was proper, Harry Heathcote at the present moment was of more importance than any other human being.

'I suppose he likes it.'

'Oh no, Mr Medlicot; how can he like it? It is not the hard work he minds, but the constant dread of coming evil.'

'The excitement keeps him alive.'

'There's plenty on a station to keep a man alive in that way at all times.'

'And plenty to keep ladies alive too?'

'Oh! ladies? I don't know that ladies have any business in the bush. Harry's trouble is all about my sister, and the children, and me. He wouldn't care a straw for himself.'

'Do you think he'd be better without a wife?'

Kate hesitated for a moment. 'Well, no. I suppose it would be very rough without Mary; and he'd be so lonely when he came in.'

'And nobody to make his tea.'

'Or to look after his things,' said Kate earnestly; 'I know it was very rough before we came here. He says that himself. There were no regular meals, but just food in a cupboard when he chose to get it.'

'That is not comfortable, certainly.'

'Horrid, I should think. I suppose it is better for him to be married. You've got your mother, Mr Medlicot.'

'Yes; I've got my mother.'

'That makes a difference, does it not?'

'A very great difference. She'll save me from having to go to a cupboard for my bread and meat.'

'I suppose having a woman about is better for a man. They haven't got anything else to do, and therefore they can look to things.'

'Do you help to look to things?'

'I suppose I do something. I often feel ashamed to think how very little it is. As for that, I'm not wanted at all.'

'So that you're free to go elsewhere?'

'I didn't mean that, Mr Medlicot; only I know I'm not of much use.'

'But if you had a house of your own?'

'Gangoil is my home just as much as it is Mary's; and I sometimes feel that Harry is just as good to me as he is to Mary.'

'Your sister will never leave Gangoil.'

'Not unless Harry gets another station.'

'But you will have to be transplanted some day.'

Kate merely chucked up her head and pouted her lips, as though to show that the proposition was one which did not deserve an answer.

'You'll marry a squatter of course, Miss Daly?'

'I don't suppose I shall ever marry anybody, Mr Medlicot.'

'You wouldn't marry any one but a squatter? I can quite understand that. The squatters here are what the lords and the country gentlemen are at home.'

'I can't even picture to myself what sort of life people live at home.'

Both Medlicot and Kate Daly meant England when they spoke of home.

'There isn't so much difference as people think. Classes hang together just in the same way; only I think there's a little more exclusiveness here than there was there.'

In answer to this Kate asserted with innocent eagerness that she was not at all exclusive, and that if ever she married any one she'd marry the man she liked.

'I wish you'd like me,' said Medlicot.

'That's nonsense,' said Kate, in a low, timid whisper, hurrying away to rejoin the other ladies. She could speculate on the delights of the beverage as would Mickey O'Dowd in his hut, but when it was first brought to her lips she could only fly away from it. In this respect Mickey O'Dowd was the more sensible of the two.

No other word was spoken that night between them, but Kate lay awake till morning, thinking of the one word that had been spoken; but the secret was kept sacredly within her own bosom.

Before the Medlicots started that night the old lady made
a proposition that the Heathcotes and Miss Daly should eat
their Christmas dinner at Medlicot's Mill. Mrs Heathcote,
thinking perhaps of her sister, thoroughly liking what she
herself had seen of the Medlicots, looked anxiously into
Harry's face. If he would consent to this an intimacy would
follow, and probably a real friendship be made.

'It's out of the question,' he said. The very firmness,
however, with which he spoke gave a certain cordiality even
to his refusal.

'I must be at home, so that the men may know where
to find me till I go out for the night.' Then after a pause
he continued, 'As we can't go to you, why should you not
come to us?'

So it was at last decided, much to Harry's own astonish-
ment, much to his wife's delight. Kate, therefore, when she
lay awake, thinking of the one word that had been spoken,
knew that there would be an opportunity for another word.

Medlicot drove his mother home safely, and, after he had
taken her into the house, encountered Nokes on his return
from Boolabong, as has been told at the close of the last
chapter.

CHAPTER VIII

'I DO WISH HE WOULD COME!'

ON the Monday morning Harry came home as usual, and as usual went to bed after his breakfast. 'I wouldn't care about the heat if it were not for the wind,' he said to his wife, as he threw himself down.

'The wind carries it so, I suppose?'

'Yes; and it comes from just the wrong side—from the north-west. There have been half a dozen fires about to-day.'

'During the night, you mean?'

'No; yesterday—Sunday. I cannot make out whether they come by themselves. They certainly are not all made by incendiaries.'

'Accidents, perhaps?'

'Well, yes. Somebody drops a match, and the sun ignites it. But the chances are much against a fire like that spreading. Care is wanted to make it spread. As far as I can learn, the worst fires have not been just after mid-day, when, of course, the heat is greater, but in the early night, before the dews have come. All the same, I feel that I know nothing about it—nothing at all. Don't let me sleep long.'

In spite of this injunction, Mrs Heathcote determined that he should sleep all day if he would. Even the nights were fearfully hot and sultry, and on this Monday morning he had come home much fatigued. He would be out again at sunset, and now he should have what rest nature would allow him. But in this resolve she was opposed by Jacko, who came in at eleven, and requested to see the master. Jacko had been over with the German, and, as he explained to Mrs Heathcote, they two had been in and out, sometimes sleeping and sometimes watching. But now he wanted to see the master, and under no persuasion would impart his information to the mistress. The poor wife, anxious as she was that her husband should sleep, did not dare in these perilous times to ignore Jacko and his information, and therefore gently woke the sleeper. In a few minutes Jacko was standing by the young squatter's bedside, and Harry Heathcote, quite awake, was sitting up and listening.

'George Brownbie's at Boolabong.' That at first was the gravamen of Jacko's news.

'I know that already, Jacko.'

'My word!' exclaimed Jacko.

In those parts Georgie Brownbie was regarded almost as the Evil One himself; and Jacko, knowing what mischief was, as it were, in the word, thought that he was entitled to bread and jam, if not to a nobbler itself, in bringing such tidings to Gangoil.

'Is that all?' asked Heathcote.

'And Bos is at Boolabong, and Bill Nokes was there all Sunday, and Jerry Brownbie's been out along with Bos and Georgie.'

'The old man wouldn't do anything of that kind, Jacko.'

'The old man! He knows nothing about it. My word! they don't tell him about nothing.'

'Or Tom?'

'Tom's away in prisin. They always cotches the best when they want to send 'em to prisin. If they'd lock up Jerry, and Georgie, and Jack! My word, yes!'

'You think they're arranging it all at Boolabong?'

'In course they are.'

'I don't see why Boscobel shouldn't be at Boolabong without intending me any harm. Of course he'd go there when he left Gangoil—that's where they all go.'

'And Bill Nokes, Mr Harry?'

'And Bill Nokes too. Though why he should travel so far from his work this weather, I can't say.'

'My word, no, Mr Harry!'

'Did you see any fires about your way last night?' Jacko shook his head. 'You go into the kitchen and get something to eat, and wait for me. I shall be out before long, now.'

Though Heathcote had made light of the assemblage of evil spirits at Boolabong, which had seemed so important to Jacko, he by no means did regard the news as unessential. Of Nokes's villany he was convinced. Of Boscobel he had imprudently made a second enemy at a most inauspicious time. Georgie Brownbie had long been his bitter foe. He had prosecuted, and perhaps persecuted, Georgie for various offences; but as Georgie was supposed to be as much at war with his own brethren as with the rest of the world at large, Heathcote had not thought much of that miscreant in the present emergency. But if the miscreant were in truth at Boolabong, and if evil things were being plotted against Gangoil, Georgie would certainly be among the conspirators.

Soon after noon Harry was on horseback and Jacko was at his heels. The heat was more intense than ever. Mrs Heathcote had twisted round Harry's hat a long white scarf, called a puggeree—though we are by no means sure of our spelling.* Jacko had spread a very dirty fragment of an old white handkerchief on his head, and wore his hat over it. Mrs Heathcote had begged Harry to take a large cotton parasol, and he had nearly consented—being unable at last to reconcile himself to the idea of riding with such an accoutrement, even in the bush.

'The heat's a bore,' he said, 'but I'm not a bit afraid of it as long as I keep moving. Yes, I'll be back to dinner, though I won't say when; and I won't say for how long. It will be the same thing all day to-morrow. I wish with all my heart those people were not coming.'

He rode straightaway to the German's hut, which was on the north-western extremity of his farther paddock in that direction. From thence the western fence ran in a southerly direction, nearly straight to the river. Beyond the fence was a strip of land, in some parts over a mile broad, in others not much over a quarter of a mile, which he claimed as belonging to Gangoil, but over which the Brownbies had driven their cattle since the fence had been made, under the pretence that the fence marked the boundary of two runs. Against this assumption Heathcote had remonstrated frequently, had driven the cattle back, and had exercised the ownership of a Crown tenant in such fashion as the nature of his occupation allowed. Beyond this strip was Boolabong, the house at Boolabong being not above three miles distant from the fence, and not above four miles from the German's hut; so that the Brownbies were in truth much nearer neighbours to the German than was Heathcote and his family. But between the German and the Brownbies there raged an internecine feud. No doubt Harry Heathcote, in his heart, liked the German all the better on this account; but it behoved him, both as a master and a magistrate, to regard reports against Boolabong coming from the German with something of suspicion. Now Jacko had been introduced to Gangoil under German auspices, and had soon come to a decision that it would be a good thing and a just to lock up all the Brownbies in the great gaol of the colony at Brisbane. He probably knew nothing of law or justice in the abstract, but he greatly valued law when exercised against those he hated. The western fence, of which mention has been made, ran down to the Mary river, hitting it about four miles west of Medlicot's Mill; so that there was a considerable portion of the Gangoil run having a frontage to the water.* As has been before said, Medlicot's plantation was about fourteen miles distant from the house at Boolabong, and the distance from the Gangoil house to that of the Brownbies was about the same.

The oppressiveness of the day was owing more to the hot wind than to the sun itself. This wind, coming from the arid plains of the interior, brought with it a dry, suffocating heat. On this occasion it was odious to Harry Heathcote, not so much on account of its own intrinsic abominations as because it might cause a fire to sweep across his run from its western boundary. Just beyond the boundary there lay Boolabong, and there were collected his enemies. A fire that should have passed for a mile or so across the pastures outside and beyond his own farm would be altogether unextinguishable by the time that it had reached his paddock. The Brownbies, as he knew well, would care nothing for burning a patch of their own grass. Their stock, if they had any at the present moment, were much too few in number to be affected by such a loss. The Brownbies had not a yard of fencing to be burned, and a fire, if once it got a hold on the edge of their run, would pass on away from them, right across Harry's pastures and Harry's fences. If such were the case, he would have quite enough to do to drive his sheep from the fire, and it might be that many of them also would perish in the flames. The catastrophe might even be so bad, so frightful, that the shed and station and all should go; though in thinking of all the fires of which he had heard, he could remember none that had spread with fatality such as that.

He found Karl Bender in his hut asleep. The man was soon up, apologizing for his somnolence, and preparing tea for his master's entertainment.

'It is not Christmas-like at home at all; is it, Mr 'Eathcote? Dear, no! Them red divils is there ready to give us a Christmas roasting.' Then he told how he had boldly ridden up to Boolabong that morning, and had seen Georgie and Boscobel with his own eyes. When asked what they had said to him, he replied that he did not wait till anything had been said, but had hurried away as fast as his horse could carry him.

'I'll go up to Boolabong myself,' said Harry.

'My word! they'll just about knock your head off!' suggested Jacko.

Karl Bender also thought that the making of such a visit would be a source of danger; but Heathcote explained that any personal attack was not to be apprehended from these men. 'That's not their game,' he said, arguing that men who premeditated a secret outrage would not probably be tempted into personal violence. The horror of the position lay in this, that though a fire should rise up almost under the feet of men who were known to be hostile to him, and whose characters were acknowledged to be bad, still would there be no evidence against them. It was known to all men that, at periods of heat such as that which was now raging, fires were common. Every day the pastures were in flames here, there, and everywhere. It was said, indeed, that there existed no evidence of fires in the bush till men had come with their flocks;* but then there had been no smoking, no boiling of pots, no camping out, till men had come—and no matches. Every one around might be sure that some particular fire had been the work of an incendiary—might be able to name the culprit who had done the deed; and yet no jury could convict the miscreant. Watchfulness was the best security—watchfulness day and night till rain should come; and Heathcote calculated that it would be better for him that his enemies should know that he was watchful. He would go up among them and show them that he was not ashamed to speak to them of his anxiety. They could hear nothing by his coming which they did not already know. They were well aware that he was on the watch, and it might be well that they should know also how close his watch was kept. He took the German and Jacko with him, but left them with their horses about a mile on the Boolabong side of his own fence, nigh to the extreme boundary of the Debateable Land. They knew his whistle, and were to ride to him at once should he call them.

He had left the house about noon, saying that he would be home to dinner, which, however, on such occasions was held to be a feast moveable over a wide space of time. But on this occasion the women expected him to come early, as it was his intention to be out again as soon as it should be dark. Mrs Growler was asked to have the dinner ready at six. During the day Mrs Heathcote was backward and forward in the kitchen. There was something wrong, she knew, but could not quite discern the evil. Sing-Sing, the cook, was more than ordinarily alert; but Sing-Sing, the cook, was not much trusted. Mrs Growler was 'as good as the Bank' as far as that went, having lived with old Mr Daly when he was prosperous; but she was apt to be down-hearted, and on the present occasion was more than usually low in spirits. Whenever Mrs Heathcote spoke she wept. At six o'clock she came into the parlour with a budget of news. Sing-Sing, the cook, had been gone for the last half-hour, leaving the leg of mutton at the fire. It soon became clear to them that he had altogether absconded.

'Them rats always does leave a falling house,' said Mrs Growler.

At seven o'clock the sun was down, though the gloom of the tropical evening had not yet come. The two ladies went out to the gate, which was but a few yards from the verandah, and there stood listening for the sound of Harry's horse. The low moaning of the wind through the trees could be heard, but it was so gentle, continuous, and unaltered, that it seemed to be no more than a vehicle for other sounds, and was as deathlike as silence itself. The gate of the horse-paddock through which Heathcote must pass on his way home was nearly a mile distant; but the road there was hard, and they knew that they could hear from there the fall of his horse's feet. There they stood from seven to nearly eight, whispering a word now and then to each other—listening always, but in vain. Looking away to the west, every now and then they fancied that they could see the sky glow with flames, and then they would tell each other that it was fancy. The evening grew darker and still darker, but no sound was heard through the moaning wind.

From time to time Mrs Growler came out to them, declaring her fears in no measured terms.

'Well, marm, I do declare I think we'd better go away out of this.'

'Go away, Mrs Growler? What nonsense! Where can we go to?'

'The mill would be nearest, ma'am, and we should be safe there. I'm sure Mrs Medlicot would take us in.'

'Why should you not be safe here?' said Kate.

'That wretched Chinese hasn't gone and left us for nothing, miss, and what would we three lone women do here if all them Brownbies came down upon us? Why don't master come back? He ought to come back; oughtn't he, ma'am? He never do think what lone women are.'

Mrs Heathcote took her husband's part very strongly, and gave Mrs Growler as hard a scolding as she knew how to pronounce. But her own courage was giving way much as Mrs Growler's had done.

'We are bound to stay here,' she said, 'and if the worst comes we must bear it as others have done before us.'

Then Mrs Growler was very sulky, and, retreating to the kitchen, sobbed there in solitude.

'Oh, Kate, I do wish he would come!' said the elder sister.

'Are you afraid?'

'It is so desolate, and he may be so far off, and we couldn't get to him if anything happened, and we shouldn't know.'

Then they were again silent, and remained without exchanging more than a word or two for nearly half an hour. They took hold of each other, and every now and then went to the kitchen door that the old woman might be comforted by their presence; but they had no consolation to offer each other. The silence of the bush, and the feeling of great distances, and the dread of calamity, almost crushed them. At last there was a distant sound of horses' feet.

'I hear him,' said Mrs Heathcote, rushing forward towards the outer gate of the horse paddock, followed by her sister.

Her ears were true, but she was doomed to disappointment. The horseman was only a messenger from her husband, Mickey O'Dowd, the Irish boundary-rider.

He had great tidings to tell, and was so long in telling them, that we will not attempt to give them in his own words. The purport of his story was as follows:—Harry had been to Boolabong House, but had found there no one but the old man. Returning home thence towards his own fence, he had smelt the smoke of fire, and had found, within a furlong of his path, a long ridge of burning grass. According to Mickey's account it could not have been lighted above a few minutes before Heathcote's presence on the spot. As it was, it had got too much ahead for him to put it out single-handed; a few yards he might have managed, but—so Mickey said, probably exaggerating the matter—there was half a quarter of a mile of flame. He had therefore ridden on before the fire, had called his own two men to him, and had at once lighted the grass himself some two hundred yards in front, making a second fire, but so keeping it down that it should be always under control. Before the hinder flames had caught him, Bender and Jacko had been with him, and they had thus managed to consume the fuel which, had it remained there, would have fed the fire which was too strong to be mastered. By watching the extremities of the line of fire, they overpowered it, and so the danger was for the moment at an end.

The method of dealing with the enemy was so well known in the bush,* and had been so often canvassed in the hearing of the two sisters, that it was clearly intelligible to them. The evil had been met in the proper way, and the remedy had been effective. But why did not Harry come home?

Mickey O'Dowd, after his fashion, explained that too. The ladies were not to wait dinner. The master felt himself obliged to remain out at night, and had gotten food at the German's hut. He, Mickey, was commissioned to return with a flask full of brandy, as it would be necessary that Harry, with all the men whom he could trust, should be 'on the rampage' all night. This small body was to consist of Harry himself, of the German, of Jacko, and, according to the story as at present told, especially of Mickey O'Dowd. Much as she would have wished to have kept the man at the station for protection, she did not think of disobeying her husband's orders. So Mickey was fed, and then sent back with the flask; with tidings also as to the desertion of that wretched cook, Sing-Sing.

'I shall sit here all night,' said Mrs Heathcote to her sister. 'As things are, I shall not think of going to bed.'

Kate declared that she would also sit in the verandah all night, and, as a matter of course, they were joined by Mrs Growler. They had been so seated about an hour, when Kate Daly declared that the heavens were on fire. The two young women jumped up, flew to the gate, and found that the whole western horizon was lurid with a dark red light.

CHAPTER IX

THE BUSH FIGHT

HARRY HEATHCOTE had, on this occasion, entertained no doubt whatever that the fire had been intentional and premeditated. A lighted torch must have been dragged along the grass, so as to ignite a line many yards long all at the same time. He had been luckily near enough to the spot to see almost the commencement of the burning, and was therefore aware of its form and circumstances. He almost wondered that he had not seen the figure of the man who had drawn the torch, or at any rate heard his steps. Pursuit would have been out of the question, as his work was wanted at the moment to extinguish the flames. The miscreant probably had remembered this, and had known that he might escape stealthily, without the noise of a rapid retreat.

When the work was over, when he had put out the fire he had himself lighted, and had exterminated the lingering remnants of that which had been intended to destroy him, he stood still awhile almost in despair. His condition seemed to be hopeless. What could he do against such a band of enemies, knowing as he did that, had he been backed even by a score of trusty followers, one foe might still suffice to ruin him? At the present moment he was very hot with the work he had done, as were also Jacko and the German. O'Dowd had also come up as they were completing their work. Their mode of extinguishing the flames had been to beat them down with branches of gum-tree loaded with leaves.* By sweeping these along the burning ground, the low flames would be scattered and expelled. But the work was very hard and hot. The boughs they used were heavy, and the air around them, sultry enough from its own properties, was made almost unbearable by the added heat of the fires.

The work had been so far done, but it might be begun again at any moment, either near or at a distance. No doubt the attempt would be made elsewhere along the boundary between Gangoil and Boolabong—was very probably being made at this moment. The two men whom he could trust and Jacko were now with him. They were wiping their brows with their arms, and panting with their work.

He first resolved on sending Mickey O'Dowd to the house. The distance was great, and the man's assistance might be essential; but he could not bear to leave his wife without news from him. Then, after considering a while, he made up his mind to go back towards his own fence, making his way as he went southerly down towards the river. They who were determined to injure him would, he thought, repeat their attempt in that direction. He hardly said a word to his two followers, but rode at a foot pace to the spot at his fence which he had selected as the site of his bivouac for the night.

'It won't be very cheery, Bender,' he said to the German; 'but we shall have to make a night of it till they disturb us again!'

The German made a motion with his arms, intended to signify his utter indifference. One place was the same as another to him. Jacko uttered his usual ejaculation, and then, having hitched his horse to the fence, threw himself on his back upon the grass.

No doubt they all slept, but they slept as watchers sleep, with one eye open. It was Harry who first saw the light which a few minutes later made itself visible to the ladies at the home station.

'Karl!' he exclaimed, jumping up, 'they're at it again—look there!'

In less than half a minute, and without speaking another word, they were all on their horses and riding in the direction of the light. It came from a part of the Boolabong run somewhat nearer to the river than the place at which they had stationed themselves, where the strip of ground between Harry's fence and the acknowledged boundary of Brownbie's run was the narrowest. As they approached the fire they became aware that it had been lighted on Boolabong. On this occasion Harry did not ride on up to the flames, knowing that the use or loss of a few minutes might save or destroy his property. He hardly spoke a word as he proceeded on his business, feeling that they upon whom he had to depend were sufficiently instructed, if only they would be sufficiently energetic.

'Keep it well under, but let it run,' was all he said, as, lighting a dried bush with a match, he ran the fire along the ground in front of the coming flames.

A stranger seeing it all would have felt sure that the remedy would have been as bad as the disease, for the fire which Harry himself made every now and again seemed to get the better of those who were endeavouring to control it. There might, perhaps, be a quarter of a mile between the front of the advancing fire and the line at which Harry had commenced to destroy the food which would have fed the coming flames. He himself, as quickly as he lighted the grass, which in itself was the work but of a moment, would strain himself to the utmost at the much harder task of controlling his own fire, so that it should not run away from him and get as it were out of his hands, and be as bad to him as that which he was thus seeking to circumvent. The German and Jacko worked like heroes, probably with intense enjoyment of the excitement, and after a while found a fourth figure among the flames, for Mickey had now returned.

'You saw them?' Harry said, panting with his work.

'They's all right,' said Mickey, flopping away with a great bough, 'but that tarnation Chinese has gone off.'

'My word! Sing-Sing. Find him at Boolabong,' said Jacko.

The German, whose gum-tree bough was a very big one, and whose every thought was intent on letting the fire run while he still held it in hand, had not breath for a syllable.

But the back fire was extending itself so as to get round them. Every now and then Harry extended his own line, moving always forward towards Gangoil as he did so, though he and his men were always on Brownbie's territory. He had no doubt but that where he could succeed in destroying the grass for a breadth of forty or fifty yards he would starve out the inimical flames. The trees and bushes without the herbage would not enable it to travel a yard. Wherever the grass was burned down black to the soil the fire would stop; but should they, who were at work, once allow themselves to be outflanked, their exertions would be all in vain. And then those wretches might light a dozen fires. The work was so hard, so hot, and often so hopeless that the unhappy young squatter was more than once tempted to bid his men desist and to return to his homestead. The flames would not follow him there. He could, at any rate, make that safe. And then, when he had repudiated this feeling as unworthy of him, he began to consider within himself whether he would not do better for his property by taking his men with him on to his run, and endeavouring to drive his sheep out of danger. But as he thought of all this he still worked, still fired the grass, and still controlled the flames. Presently he became aware of what seemed to him at first to be a third fire. Through the trees, in the direction of the river, he could see the glimmering of low flames, and the figures of men. But it was soon apparent to him that these men were working in his cause, and that they, too, were burning the grass that would have fed the advancing flames. At first he could not spare the minute which would be necessary to find out who was his friend, but as they drew nearer he knew the man. It was the sugar planter from the Mill, and with him his foreman.

'We've been doing our best,' said Medlicot, 'but we've been terribly afraid that the fire would slip away from us.'

'It's the only thing,' said Harry, too much excited at the moment to ask questions as to the cause of Medlicot's presence so far from his home at that time in the evening. 'It's getting round us, I'm afraid, all the same.'

'I don't know but it is. It's almost impossible to distinguish. How hot the fires make it!'

'Hot, indeed,' said Harry. 'It's killing work for men, and then all for no good! To think that men—creatures that call themselves men—should do such a thing as this! It breaks one's heart.'

He had paused as he spoke, leaning on the great battered bough which he held, but in an instant was at work with it again.

'Do you stay here, Mr Medlicot, with the men, and I'll go on beyond where you began. If I find the fire growing down I'll shout and they can come to me.' So saying he rushed on with a lighted bush-torch in his hand.

Suddenly he found himself confronted in the bush by a man on horseback, whom he at once recognized as Georgie Brownbie. He forgot for a moment where he was, and began to question the reprobate as to his presence at that spot.

'That's like your impudence!' said Georgie. 'You're not only trespassing, but you're destroying our property wilfully, and you ask me what business I have here. You're a nice sort of young man!'

Harry, checked for a moment by the remembrance that he was in truth upon Boolabong run, did not at once answer.

'Put that bush down and don't burn our grass,' continued Georgie, 'or you shall have to answer for it. What right have you to fire our grass?'

'Who fired it first?'

'It lighted itself. That's no rule why you should light it more. You give over, or I'll punch your head for you!'

Harry's men and Medlicot were advancing towards him, trampling out their own embers as they came, and Georgie Brownbie, who was alone, when he saw that there were four or five men against him, turned round and rode back.

'Did you ever see impudence like that?' said Harry. 'He is probably the very man who set the match, and yet he comes and brazens it out with me!'

'I don't think he's the man who set the match,' said Medlicot quietly; 'at any rate there was another.'

'Who was it?'

'My man Nokes. I saw him with the torch in his hand.'

'Heaven and earth!'

'Yes, Mr Heathcote; I saw him put it down. You were about right, you see, and I was about wrong.'

Harry had not a word to say, unless it were to tell the man that he loved him for the frankness of his confession; but the moment was hardly auspicious for such a declaration. There was no excuse for them to pause in their work, for the fire was still crackling at their back, and they did no more than pause. 'Ah!' said Harry, 'there it goes! We shall be done at last;' for he saw that he was being outflanked by the advancing flames. But still they worked, drawing lines of fire here and there, and still they hoped that there might be ground for hope. Nokes had been seen; but, pregnant as the theme might be with words, it was almost impossible to talk. Questions could not be asked and answered without stopping in their toil. There were questions which Harry longed to ask. Could Medlicot swear to the man? Did the man know that he had been seen? If he knew that he had been watched whilst he lit the grass, he would soon be far away from Medlicot's Mill and Gangoil. Harry felt that it would be a consolation to him in his trouble if he could get hold of this man, and keep him, and prosecute him, and have him hung. Even in the tumult of the moment he was able to reflect about it, and to think that he remembered that the crime of arson was capital in the colony of Queensland.* He had endeavoured to be good to the men with whom he had dealings. He had not stinted their food, or cut them short in their wages, or been hard in exacting work from them. And this was his return! Ideas as to the excellence of absolute dominion and power flitted across his brain—such power as Abraham no doubt exercised.* In Abraham's time the people were submissive and the world was happy. Harry Heathcote, at least, had never heard that it was not happy. But as he thought of all this he worked away with his bush and his matches—extinguishing the flames here and lighting them there—striving to make a cordon of black bare ground between Boolabong and Gangoil. Surely Abraham had never been called on to work like this!

He and his men were in a line, covering something above a quarter of a mile of ground, of which line he was himself the nearest to the river, and Medlicot and his foreman the farthest from it. The German and O'Dowd were in the middle, and Jacko was working with his master. If Harry had just cause for anger and sorrow in regard to Nokes and Boscobel, he certainly had equal cause to be proud of the staunchness of his remaining satellites. The men worked with a will, as though the whole run had been the personal property of each of them. Nokes and Boscobel would probably have done the same had the fires come before they had quarrelled with their master. It is a small and narrow point that turns the rushing train to the right or to the left. The rushing man is often turned off by a point as small and narrow.

'My word!' said Jacko, on a sudden; 'here they are all o' horseback!' And as he spoke there was the sound of half a dozen horsemen galloping up to them through the bush. 'Why, there's Bos, his own self!' said Jacko.

The two leading men were Joe and Jerry Brownbie, who for this night only had composed their quarrels, and close to them was Boscobel. There were others behind, also mounted—Jack Brownbie and Georgie, and Nokes himself. But they, though their figures were seen, could not be distinguished in the gloom of the night; nor, indeed, did Harry at first discern of how many the party consisted. It seemed that there was a whole troop of horsemen, whose purpose it was to interrupt him in his work, so that the flames should certainly go ahead. And it was evident that the men thought that they could do so without subjecting themselves to legal penalties. As far as Harry Heathcote could see, they were correct in their view. He could have no right to burn the grass on Boolabong. He had no claim even to be there. It was true that he could plead that he was stopping the fire which they had purposely made; but they could prove his handiwork, whereas it would be almost impossible that he should prove theirs.

The whole forest was not red, but lurid, with the fires, and the air was laden with both the smell and the heat of the conflagration. The horsemen were dressed, as was Harry himself, in trousers and shirts, with old slouch hats, and each of them had a cudgel in his hand. As they came galloping up through the trees, they were as uncanny and unwelcome a set of visitors as any man was ever called on to receive. Harry necessarily stayed his work, and stood still to bear the brunt of the coming attack; but Jacko went on with his employment faster than ever, as though a troop of men in the dark were nothing to him.

Jerry Brownbie was the first to speak. 'What's this you're up to, Heathcote? Firing our grass? It's arson. You shall swing for this!'

'I'll take my chance of that,' said Harry, turning to his work again.

'No! I'm blessed if you do! Ride over him, Bos, while I stop these other fellows!'

The Brownbies had been aware that Harry's two boundary-riders were with him, but had not heard of the arrival of Medlicot and the other man. Nokes was aware that some one on horseback had been near him when he was firing the grass, but had thought that it was one of the party from Gangoil. By the time that Jerry Brownbie had reached the German, Medlicot was there also.

'Who the deuce are you?' asked Jerry.

'What business is that of yours?' said Medlicot.

'No business of mine, and you firing our grass! I'll let you know my business pretty quickly!'

'It's that fellow Medlicot, from the sugar-mill,' said Joe; 'the man that Nokes is with.'

'I thought you was a horse of another colour,' continued Jerry, who had been given to understand that Medlicot was Heathcote's enemy. 'Any way, I won't have my grass fired. If God A'mighty chooses to send fires, we can't help it; but I'm not going to have incendiaries here as well. You're a new chum, and don't understand what you're about, but you must stop this.'

As Medlicot still went on putting out the fire, Jerry attempted to ride him down. Medlicot caught the horse by the rein and violently backed the brute in among the embers. The animal plunged and reared, getting his head loose, and at last came down, he and his rider together. In the meantime Joe Brownbie, seeing this, rode up behind the sugar-planter, and struck him violently with his cudgel over the shoulder. Medlicot sank nearly to the ground, but at once recovered himself. He knew that some bone on the left side of his body was broken; but he could still fight with his right hand—and he did fight.

Boscobel and Georgie Brownbie both attempted to ride over Harry together, and might have succeeded, had not Jacko ingeniously inserted the burning branch of gum-tree with which he had been working under the belly of the horse on which Boscobel was riding. The animal jumped immediately from the ground, bucking into the air, and Boscobel was thrown far over his head. Georgie Brownbie then turned upon Jacko, but Jacko was far too nimble to be caught, and escaped among the trees.

For a few minutes the fight was general, but the footmen had the best of it, in spite of the injury done to Medlicot. Jerry was bruised and burned about the face by his fall among the ashes, and did not much relish the work afterwards. Boscobel was stunned for a few moments, and was quite ready to retreat when he came to himself. Nokes during the whole time did not show himself, alleging as a reason afterwards the presence of his employer, Medlicot.

'I'm blessed if your cowardice shan't hang you!' said Joe Brownbie to him on their way home. 'Do you think we're going to fight the battles of a fellow like you, who hasn't pluck to come forward himself?'

'I've as much pluck as you,' answered Nokes, 'and am ready to fight you any day. But I know when a man is to come forward and when he's not. Hang me! I'm not so near hanging as some folks at Boolabong.'

We may imagine therefore that the night was not spent pleasantly among the Brownbies after these adventures.

There was, of course, very much cursing and swearing, and very many threats before the party from Boolabong did retreat. Their great point was of course this—that Heathcote was wilfully firing the grass, and was, therefore, no better than an incendiary. Of course they stoutly denied that the original fire had been intentional, and denied as stoutly that the original fire could be stopped by fires. But at last they went, leaving Heathcote and his party masters of the battle-field. Jerry was taken away in a sad condition; and in subsequent accounts of the transaction given from Boolabong, his fall was put forward as the reason of their flight, he having been the general on the occasion. And Boscobel had certainly lost all stomach for immediate fighting. Immediately behind the battle-field they came across Nokes, and Sing-Sing the runaway cook from Gangoil. The

poor Chinaman had made the mistake of joining the party
which was not successful.

But Harry, though the victory was with him, was hardly
in a mood for triumph. He soon found that Medlicot's
collar-bone was broken, and it would be necessary, therefore, that he should return with the wounded man to the
station. And the flames, as he feared, had altogether got
ahead of him during the fight. As far as they had gone they
had stopped the fire, having made a black wilderness a mile
and a half in length, which, during the whole distance,
ceased suddenly at the line at which the subsidiary fire had
been extinguished. But, while the attack was being made
upon them, the flames had crept on to the southward, and
had now got beyond their reach. It had seemed, however,
that the mass of fire which had got away from them was
small, and already the damp of the night was on the grass;
and Harry felt himself justified in hoping, not that there
might be no loss, but that the loss might not be ruinous.

Medlicot consented to be taken back to Gangoil instead
of to the mill. Perhaps he thought that Kate Daly might
be a better nurse than his mother, or that the quiet of the
sheep station might be better for him than the clatter of
his own mill-wheels. It was midnight, and they had a ride
of fourteen miles, which was hard enough upon a man with
a broken collar-bone. The whole party also was thoroughly
fatigued. The work they had been doing was about as hard
as could fall to a man's lot, and they had now been many
hours without food. Before they started, Mickey produced
his flask, the contents of which were divided equally among
them all, including Jacko.

As they were preparing to start home, Medlicot explained
that it had struck him by degrees that Heathcote might be
right in regard to Nokes, and that he had determined to
watch the man himself whenever he should leave the mill.
On that Monday he had given up work somewhat earlier
than usual, saying that, as the following day was Christ-

mas,* he should not come to the mill. From that time Medlicot and his foreman had watched him.

'Yes,' said he, in answer to a question from Heathcote; 'I can swear that I saw him with the lighted torch in his hand, and that he placed it among the grass. There were two others from Boolabong with him, and they must have seen him too.'

CHAPTER X

HARRY HEATHCOTE RETURNS IN TRIUMPH

WHEN the fight was quite over, and Heathcote's party had
returned to their horses, Medlicot for a few minutes was
faint and sick, but he revived after a while, and declared
himself able to sit on his horse. There was a difficulty in
getting him up, but when there, he made no further
complaint.

'This,' said he, as he settled himself in his saddle, 'is my
first Christmas Day in Australia. I landed early in January,
and last year I was on my way home to fetch my mother.'

'It's not much like an English Christmas,' said Harry.

'Nor yet as in Hanover,' said the German.

'It's Cork you should go to, or Galway, bedad, if you
want to see Christmas kep' after the ould fashion,' said
Mickey.

'I think we used to do it pretty well in Cumberland,' said
Medlicot. 'There are things which can't be transplanted.
They may roast beef, and all that, but you should have
cold weather to make you feel that it is Christmas indeed.'

'We do it as well as we can,' Harry pleaded. 'I've seen
a great pudding come into the room all afire—just to
remind one of the old country—when it has been so hot
that one could hardly bear a shirt on one's shoulders. But
yet there's something in it. One likes to think of the old
place, though one is so far away. How do you feel now?
Does the jolting hurt you much? If your horse is rough,
change with me. This fellow goes as smooth as a lady.'

Medlicot declared that the pain did not trouble him
much.

'They'd have ridden over us, only for you,' continued
Harry.

'My word! wouldn't they?' said Jacko, who was very proud of his own part in the battle. 'I say, Mr Medlicot, did you see Bos and his horse part company? You did, Mr Harry. Didn't he fly like a bird, all in among the bushes? I owed Bos one—I did, my word!—and now I've paid him.'

'I saw it,' said Harry. 'He was riding at me as hard as he could come. I can't understand Boscobel. Nokes is a sly, bad, slinging fellow, whom I never liked. But I was always good to Bos; and when he cheated me, as he did, about his time, I never even threatened to stop his money.'

'You told him of it too plain,' said the German.

'I did tell him—of course—as I should you. It has come to that now, that if a man robs you—your own man—you are not to dare to tell him of it! What would you think of me, Karl, if I were to find you out and was to be afraid of speaking to you, lest you should turn against me and burn my fences?'

Karl Bender shrugged his shoulders, holding his reins up to his eyes.

'I know what you ought to think! And I wish that every man about Gangoil should be sure that I will always say what I think right. I don't know that I ever was hard upon any man. I try not to be.'

'Thrue for you, Mr Harry,' said the Irishman.

'I'm not going to pick my words because men like Nokes and Boscobel have the power of injuring me. I'm not going to truckle to rascals because I'm afraid of them. I'd sooner be burned out of house and home, and go and work on the wharves in Brisbane than that.'

'My word! yes,' said Jacko, 'and I too.'

'If the devil is to get ahead he must, but I won't hold a candle to him. You fellows may tell every man about the place what I say. As long as I'm master of Gangoil I'll be master, and when I come across a swindle I'll tell the man who does it he's a swindler. I told Bos to his face; but I didn't tell anybody else, and I shouldn't if he'd taken it right and mended his ways.'

They all understood him very well—the German, the Irishman, Medlicot's foreman, Medlicot himself, and even Jacko; and, though, no doubt, there was a feeling within the hearts of the men that Harry Heathcote was imperious, still they respected him—and they believed him.

'The masther should be the masther, no doubt,' said the Irishman.

'A man that is a man vill not sell hisself body and soul,' said the German slowly.

'Do I want dominion over your soul, Karl Bender?' asked the squatter with energy. 'You know I don't, nor over your body, except so far as it suits you to sell your services. What you sell you part with readily—like a man; and it's not likely that you and I shall quarrel. But all this row about nothing can't be very pleasant to a man with a broken shoulder.'

'I like to hear you,' said Medlicot. 'I'm always a good listener when men have something really to say.'

'Well, then—I've something to say,' cried Harry. 'There never was a man came to my house whom I'd sooner see as a Christmas guest than yourself.'

'Thankee, sir.'

'It's more than I could have said yesterday with truth.'

'It's more than you did say.'

'Yes, by George! But you've beat me now. When you're hard pressed for hands down yonder, you send for me and see if I won't turn the mill for you—or hoe canes either.'

'So 'll I—my word, yes!—just for my rations.'

They had by this time reached the Gangoil fence, having taken the directest route for the house. But Harry in doing this had not been unmindful of the fire. Had Medlicot not been wounded he would have taken the party somewhat out of the way, down southwards, following the flames; but Medlicot's condition had made him feel that he would not be justified in doing so. Now, however, it occurred to him, that he might as well ride a mile or two down the fence, and see what injury had been done. The escort of the men would be sufficient to take Medlicot to the station, and he would reach the place as soon as they. If the flames were still running ahead, he knew that he could not now stop them, but he could at least learn how the matter stood with him. If the worst came to the worst he would not now lose more than three or four miles of fencing and the grass off a corner of his run. Nevertheless, tired as he was, he could not bear the idea of going home without knowing the whole story. So he made his proposal. Medlicot, of course, made no objection. Each of the men offered to go with him, but he declined their services.

'There is nothing to do,' said he, 'and nobody to catch; and if the fire is burning it must burn.'

So he went alone.

The words that he had uttered among his men had not been lightly spoken. He had begun to perceive that life would be very hard to him in his present position, or perhaps altogether impossible, as long as he was at enmity with all those around him. Old squatters whom he knew, respectable men who had been in the colony before he was born, had advised him to be on good terms with the Brownbies. 'You needn't ask them to your house, or go to them—but just soft-sawder them when you meet,' an old gentleman had said to him. He certainly hadn't taken the old gentleman's advice—thinking that to 'soft-sawder' so great a reprobate as Jerry Brownbie would be holding a candle to the devil. But his own plan had hardly answered. Well, he was sure at any rate of this—that he could do no good now by endeavouring to be civil to the Brownbies. He soon came to the place where the fire had reached his fence, and found that it had burned its way through, and that the flames were still continuing their onward course. The fence to the north—or rather to the north-westward, the point whence the wind was coming—stood firm at the spot at which the fire had struck it. Dry as the wood was, the flames had not travelled upwards against the wind; but to the south the fire was travelling down the fence. To stop this he rode half a mile along the burning barrier till he had headed the flames, and then he pulled the bushes down and rolled away the logs, so as to stop the destruction. As regarded his fence, there was less than a mile of it destroyed, and that he could now leave in security, as the wind was blowing away from it. As for his grass, that must now take its chance. He could see the dark light of the low running fire, but there was no longer a mighty blaze, and he knew that the dew of the night was acting as his protector. The harm that had been as yet done was trifling, if only he could protect himself from further harm. After leaving the fire he had still a ride of seven or eight miles through the gloom of the forest—all alone. Not only was he weary, but his horse was so tired that he could hardly get him to canter for a furlong. He regretted that he had not brought the boy with him, knowing well the service of companionship to a tired beast. He was used to such troubles, and could always tell himself that his back was broad enough to bear them; but his desolation among enemies oppressed him. Medlicot, however, was no longer an enemy. Then there came across his mind for the first time an idea that Medlicot might marry his sister-in-law, and become his fast friend. If he could have but one true friend he thought that he could bear the enmity of all the Brownbies. Hitherto he had been entirely alone in his anxiety. It was between three and four when he reached Gangoil, and he found that the party of horsemen had just entered the yard before him. The sugar planter was so weak that he could hardly get off his horse.

The two ladies were still watching when the cavalcade arrived, though it was then between three and four in the morning. It was Harry's custom on such occasions to ride up to the little gate close to the verandah, and there to hang his bridle till some one should take his horse away; but on this occasion he and the others rode into the yard. Seeing this, Mrs Heathcote and her sister went through the house, and soon learned how things were. Mr Medlicot from the mill had come with a bone broken, and it was their duty to nurse him till a doctor could be procured from Maryborough. Now, Maryborough was thirty miles distant. Some one must be despatched at once. Jacko volunteered, but in such a service Jacko was hardly to be trusted. He might fall asleep on his horse and continue his slumbers on the ground. Mickey and the German both offered; but the men were so beaten by their work that Heathcote did not dare to take their offer.

'I'll tell you what it is, Mary,' he said to his wife, 'there is nothing for it but for me to go for Jackson;'—Jackson was the doctor—'and I can see the police at the same time.'

'You shan't go, Harry. You are so tired already you can hardly stand this moment.'

'Get me some strong coffee—at once. You don't know what that man has done for us. I'll tell you all another time. I owe him more than a ride into Maryborough. I'll make the men get Yorkie up'—Yorkie was a favourite horse he had—'while you make the coffee; and I'll lead Colonel'—Colonel was another horse well esteemed at Gangoil. 'Jackson will come quicker on him than on any animal he can get at Maryborough.' And so it was arranged, in spite of the wife's tears and entreaties. Harry had his coffee and some food, and started with his two horses for the doctor.

Nature is so good to us that we are sometimes disposed to think we might have dispensed with art. In the bush, where doctors cannot be had, bones will set themselves; and when doctors do come, but come slowly, the broken bones suit themselves to such tardiness. Medlicot was brought in and put to bed. Let the reader not be shocked to hear that Kate Daly's room was given up to him, as

being best suited for a sick man's comfort; and the two
ladies took it in turn to watch him. Mrs Heathcote was, of
course, the first, and remained with him till dawn. Then
Kate crept to the door, and asked whether she should
relieve her sister. Medlicot was asleep, and it was agreed
that Kate should remain in the verandah, and look in from
time to time, to see whether the wounded man required
aught at her hands. She looked in very often, and then, at
last, he was awake. 'Miss Daly,' he said, 'I feel so ashamed
of the trouble I'm giving.'

'Don't speak of it. It is nothing. In the bush everybody,
of course, does anything for everybody.' When the words
were spoken she felt that they were not as complimentary
as she would have wished. 'You were to have come to-day,
you know, but we did not think you'd come like this, did
we?'

'I don't know why I didn't go home instead of coming
here.'

'The doctor will reach Gangoil sooner than he could the
mill. You are better here, and we will send for Mrs Medlicot
as soon as the men have had a rest. How was it all, Mr
Medlicot? Harry says that there was a fight, and that you
came in just at the nick of time, and that but for you all
the run would have been burned.'

'Not that at all.'

'He said so; only he went off so quickly, and was so busy
with things, that we hardly understood him. Is it not
dreadful that there should be such fighting? And then these
horrid fires! You were in the middle of the fire, were you
not?' It suited Kate's feelings that Medlicot should be the
hero of this occasion.

'We were lighting them in front to put them out behind.'

'And then, while you were at work, these men from
Boolabong came upon you. Oh, Mr Medlicot, we shall be
so very, very wretched if you are much hurt! My sister is
so unhappy about it.'

'It's only my collar-bone, Miss Daly.'

'But that is so dreadful.'

She was still thinking of the one word he had spoken when he had—well, not asked her for her love, but said that which between a young man and a young woman ought to mean the same thing. Perhaps it had meant nothing? She had heard that young men do say things which mean nothing. But to her, living in the solitude of Gangoil, the one word had been so much! Her heart had melted with absolute acknowledged love when the man had been brought through into the house with all the added attraction of a broken bone. While her sister had watched, she had retired—to rest, as Mary had said, but in truth to think of the chance which had brought her in this guise into familiar contact with the man she loved. And then, when she had crept up to take her place in watching him, she had almost felt that shame should restrain her. But it was her duty; and, of course, a man with a collar-bone broken would not speak of love.

'It will make your Christmas so sad for you!' he said.

'Oh, as for that, we mind nothing about it—for ourselves. We are never very gay here.'

'But you are happy?'

'Oh, yes, quite happy—except when Harry is disturbed by these troubles. I don't think anybody has so many troubles as a squatter. It sometimes seems that all the world is against him.'

'We shall be allies now, at any rate.'

'Oh, I do so hope we shall!' said Kate, putting her hands together in her energy, and then retreating from her energy with sad awkwardness when she remembered the personal application of her wish. 'That is, I mean you and Harry,' she added in a whisper.

'Why not I and others besides Harry?'

'It is so much to him to have a real friend. Things concern us, of course, only just as they concern him.

Women are never of very much account, I think. Harry
has to do everything, and everything ought to be done for
him.'

'I think you spoil Harry among you.'

'Don't you say so to Mary, or she will be fierce.'

'I wonder whether I shall ever have a wife to stand up
for me in that way?' Kate had no answer to make, but she
thought that it would be his own fault if he did not have
a wife to stand up for him thoroughly. 'He has been very
lucky in his wife?'

'I think he has, Mr Medlicot; but you are moving about,
and you ought to lie still. There! I hear the horses; that's
the doctor. I do so hope he won't say that anything very
bad is the matter.' She jumped up from her chair, which
was close to his bed, and, as she did so, just touched his
hand with hers. It was involuntary on her part, having come
of instinct rather than will, and she withdrew herself instantly. The hand she had touched belonged to the arm
that was not hurt, and he put it out after her, and caught
her by the sleeve as she was retreating. 'Oh, Mr Medlicot,
you must not do that; you will hurt yourself if you move
in that way.' And so she escaped, and left the room, and
did not see him again till the doctor had gone from
Gangoil.

The bone had been broken simply as other bones are
broken; it was now set, and the sufferer was, of course, told
that he must rest. He had suggested that he should be taken
home, and the Heathcotes had concurred with the doctor
in asserting that no proposition could be more absurd. He
had intended to eat his Christmas dinner at Gangoil, and
he must now pass his entire Christmas there.

'The sugar can go on very well for ten days,' Harry had
said; 'I'll go over myself and see about the men, and I'll
fetch your mother over.'

To this, however, Mrs Heathcote had demurred success-
fully. 'You'll kill yourself, Harry, if you go on like this,' she

said. Bender, therefore, was sent in the buggy for the old lady, and at last Harry Heathcote consented to go to bed.

'My belief is I shall sleep for a week,' he said as he turned in. But he didn't begin his sleep quite at once. 'I am very glad I went into Maryborough,' he said to his wife, rising up from his pillow. 'I've sworn an information against Nokes and two of the Brownbies, and the police will be after them this afternoon. They won't catch Nokes, and they can't convict the other fellows. But it will be something to clear the country of such a fellow, and something also to let them know that detection is possible.'

'Do sleep now, dear!' she said.

'Yes, I will; I mean to. But look here, Mary; if any of the police should come here, mind you wake me at once. And Mary, look here; do you know I shouldn't be a bit surprised if that fellow was to be making up to Kate?'

Mrs Heathcote, with some little inward chuckle at her husband's assumed quickness of apprehension, reminded herself that the same idea had occurred to her some time ago. Mrs Heathcote gave her husband full credit for more than ordinary intelligence in reference to affairs appertaining to the breeding of sheep and the growing of wool, but she did not think highly of his discernment in such an affair as this. She herself had been much quicker. When she first saw Mr Medlicot she had felt it a God-send that such a man, with the look of a gentleman, and unmarried, should come into the neighbourhood; and in so feeling her heart had been entirely with her sister. For herself it mattered nothing who came or did not come, or whether a man were a bachelor or possessed of a wife and a dozen children. All that a girl had a right to want was a good husband. She was quite satisfied with her own lot in that respect, but she was anxious enough on behalf of Kate. And when a young man did come, who might make matters so pleasant for them, Harry quarrelled with him because he was a free-selector!

'A free fiddlestick!' she had once said to Kate—not, however, communicating to her innocent sister the ambition which was already filling her own bosom. 'Harry does take things up so, as though people weren't to live, some in one way and some in another! As far as I can see, Mr Medlicot is a very nice fellow.'

Kate had remarked that he was 'all very well,' and nothing more had been said; but Mrs Heathcote, in spite of Harry's aversion, had formed her little project—a project which, if then declared, would have filled Harry with dismay. And now the young aristocrat, as he turned himself in his bed, made the suggestion to his wife as though it were all his own!

'I never like to think much of these things beforehand,' she said innocently.

'I don't know about thinking,' said Harry; 'but a girl might do worse. If it should come up, don't set yourself against it.'

'Kate, of course, will please herself,' said Mrs Heathcote. 'Now do lie down and rest yourself!'

His rest, however, was not of long duration. As he had himself suggested, two policemen reached Gangoil at about three in the afternoon on their way from Maryborough to Boolabong, in order that they might take Mr Medlicot's deposition. After Heathcote's departure it had occurred to Sergeant Forrest, of the police—and the suggestion, having been transferred from the sergeant to the stipendiary magistrate, was now produced with magisterial sanction—that after all there was no evidence against the Brownbies. They had simply interfered to prevent the burning of the grass on their own run, and who could say that they had committed any crime by doing so? If Medlicot had seen Nokes with a lighted branch in his hand, the matter might be different with him; and therefore Medlicot's deposition was taken. He had sworn that he had seen Nokes drag his lighted torch along the ground; he had also seen other

horsemen—two or three, as he thought—but could not
identify them. Jacko's deposition was also taken as to the
man who had been heard and seen in the wool-shed at
night. Jacko was ready to swear point blank that the man
was Nokes. The policemen suggested that, as the night was
dark, Jacko might as well allow a shade of doubt to appear,
thinking that the shade of doubt would add strength to the
evidence. But Jacko was not going to be taught what sort
of oath he should swear. 'My word!' he said. 'Didn't I see
his leg move? You go away!'

Armed with these depositions, the two constables went
on to Boolabong in search of Nokes, and of Nokes only,
much to the chagrin of Harry, who declared that the police
would never really bestir themselves in a squatter's cause.
'As for Nokes, he'll be out of Queensland by this time
to-morrow.'

CHAPTER XI

SERGEANT FORREST

THE Brownbie party returned, after their midnight raid, in great discomfiture to Boolabong. Their leader, Jerry, was burned about his hands and face in a disagreeable and unsightly manner; Joe had hardly made good that character for 'fighting it out to the end,' for which he was apt to claim credit; Boscobel was altogether disconcerted by his fall; and Nokes, who had certainly shown no aptitude for the fray, was abused by them all as having caused their retreat by his cowardice; while Sing-Sing, the runaway cook, who knew that he had forfeited his wages at Gangoil, was forced to turn over in his heathenish mind the ill-effects of joining the losing side. 'You big fool, Bos,' he said more than once to his friend the woodsman, who had lured him away from the comforts of Gangoil. 'I'll punch your head, John,* if you don't hold your row,' Boscobel would reply. But Sing-Sing went on with his reproaches, and, before they had reached Boolabong, Boscobel had punched the Chinaman's head.

'You're not coming in here,' Jerry said to Nokes, when they reached the yard gate.

'Who wants to come in? I suppose you're not going to send a fellow on without a bit of grub after such a night's work?'

'Give him some bread and meat, Jack, and let him go on. There'll be somebody here after him before long. He can't hurt us, but I don't want people to think that we are so fond of him that we can't do without harbouring him here. Georgie, you'll go too, if you take my advice. That young cur will send the police here as sure as my name is Brownbie, and if they once get hold of you, they'll have a great many things to talk to you about.'

Georgie grumbled when he heard this, but he knew that the advice given him was good, and he did not attempt to enter the house. So Nokes and he vanished away into the bush together—as such men do vanish—wandering forth to live as the wild beasts live. It was still a dark night when they went, and the remainder of the party took themselves to their beds.

On the following afternoon they were lying about the house, sometimes sleeping and sometimes waking up to smoke, when the two policemen, who had already been at Gangoil, appeared in the yard. These men were dressed in flat caps, with short blue jackets, hunting breeches, and long black boots, very unlike any policeman in the old country, and much more picturesque. They leisurely tied their horses up, as though they had been in the habit of making weekly visits to the place, and walked round to the verandah.

'Well, Mr Brownbie, and how are you?' said the sergeant to the old man.

The head of the family was gracious, and declared himself to be pretty well, considering all things. He called the sergeant by his name, and asked the men whether they'd take a bit of something to eat. Joe also was courteous, and, after a little delay in getting a key from his brother, brought out the jar of spirits—which, in the bush, is regarded as the best sign known of thorough good breeding. The sergeant said that he didn't mind if he did; and the other man, of course, followed his officer's example.

So far everything was comfortable, and the constables seemed in no hurry to allude to disagreeable subjects. They condescended to eat a bit of cold meat before they proceeded to business. And at last the matter to be discussed was first introduced by one of the Brownbie family.

'I suppose you've heard that there was a scrimmage here last night?' said Joe.

The Brownbie party present consisted of the old man, Joe and Jack Brownbie, and Boscobel—Jerry keeping himself in the background because of his disfigurement. The sergeant, as he swallowed his food, acknowledged that he had heard something about it.

'And that's what brings you here?' continued Joe.

'There ain't nothing wrong here,' said old Brownbie.

'I hope not, Mr Brownbie,' said the sergeant. 'I hope not. We haven't got anything against you, at any rate.'

Sergeant Forrest was a graduate of Oxford, the son of an English clergyman, who, having his way to make in the world, had thought that an early fortune would be found in the colonies. He had come out, had failed, had suffered some very hard things, and now, at the age of thirty-five, enjoyed life thoroughly as a sergeant of the colonial police.

'You haven't got anything against anybody here, I should think?' said Joe.

'If you want to get them as begun it,' said Jack, 'and them as ought to be took up, you'll go to Gangoil.'

'Hold your tongue, Jack!' said his brother. 'Sergeant Forrest knows where to go better than you can tell him.'

Then the sergeant asked a string of questions as to the nature of the fight; who had been hurt; and how badly had anybody been hurt; and what other harm had been done. The answers to all these questions were given with a fair amount of truth, except that the little circumstance of the origin of the fire was not explained. Both Boscobel and Joe had seen the torch put down, but it could hardly have been expected that they should have been explicit as to such a detail as that. Nor did they mention the names of either their brother George or Nokes.

'And who was there in the matter?' asked the sergeant.

'There was young Heathcote, and a boy he has got there, and the two chaps as he calls boundary-riders, and Medlicot, the sugar fellow from the mill, and a chap of Medlicot's I never set eyes on before. They must have expected something to be up, or Heathcote would not have been going about at night with a tribe of men like that.'

'And who were your party?'

'Well, there were just ourselves, four of us, for Georgie was here, and this fellow Boscobel. Georgie never stays long, and he wouldn't be welcome if he did. He turned up just by chance like, and now he's off again.'

'That was all, eh?'

Of course, they all knew that the sergeant knew that Nokes had been with them.

'Well, then, that wasn't all,' said old Brownbie. 'Bill Nokes was here, whom Heathcote dismissed ever so long ago. And that Chinese cook of his. He dismissed him too, I suppose. And he dismissed Boscobel here.'

'No one can live at Gangoil any time,' said Jack. 'Everybody knows that. He wants to be lord a'mighty over everything; but he ain't going to be lord a'mighty at Boolabong.'

'And he ain't going to burn our grass either,' said Joe. 'It's like his impudence coming on to our run and burning everything before him. He calls hisself a magistrate, but he's not to do just as he pleases because he's a magistrate. I suppose we can swear against him for lighting our grass, sergeant? There isn't one of us that didn't see him do it.'

'And where is Nokes?' asked the sergeant, paying no attention to the application made by Mr Brownbie, junior, for redress to himself.

'Well,' said Joe, 'Nokes isn't anywhere about Boolabong.'

'He's away with your brother George?'

'I shouldn't wonder,' said Joe.

'It's a serious matter lighting a fire, you know,' said the sergeant. 'A man would have to swing for it.'

'Then why isn't young Heathcote to swing?' demanded Jack.

'There is such a thing as intent, you know. When Heathcote lighted the fire, where would the fire have gone if he hadn't kept putting it out as fast as he kept lighting it? On to his own run; not to yours. And where would the other fire have gone which somebody lit, and which nobody put out, if he hadn't been there to stop it? The less you say against Heathcote the better. So Nokes is off, is he?'

'He ain't here, anyways,' said Joe. 'When the row was over we wouldn't let him in. We didn't want him about here.'

'I dare say not,' said the sergeant. 'Now let me go and see the spot where the fight was.'

So the two policemen, with the two young Brownbies, rode away, leaving Boscobel with the old man.

'He knows everything about it,' said old Brownbie.

'If he do,' said Boscobel, 'it ain't no odds.'

'Not a ha'porth of odds,' said Jerry, coming out of his hiding-place. 'Who cares what he knows? A man may do what he pleases on his own run, I suppose?'

'He mayn't light a fire as 'll spread,' said the old man.

'Bother! Who's to prove what's in a man's mind? If I'd been Nokes I'd have stayed and seen it out. I'd never be driven about the colony by such a fellow as Heathcote, with all the police in the world to back him.'

Sergeant Forrest inspected the ground on which the fire had raged, and the spot on which the men had met; but nothing came of his inspection, and he had not expected that anything would come of it. He could see exactly where the fire had commenced, and could trace the efforts that had been made to stop it. He did not in the least doubt the way in which it had been lit; but he did very much doubt whether a jury could find Nokes guilty, even if he could catch Nokes. Jacko's evidence was worth nothing, and Mr Medlicot might be easily mistaken as to what he had seen at a distance in the middle of the night.

All this happened on Christmas Day. At about nine o'clock the same evening the two constables reappeared at Gangoil, and asked for hospitality for the night. This was a matter of course, and also the reproduction of the Christmas dinner. Mrs Medlicot was now there; and her son, with his collar-bone set, had been allowed to come out on to the verandah. The house had already been supposed to be full; but room, as a matter of course, was made for Sergeant Forrest and his man.

'It's a queer sort of Christmas we've all been having, Mr Heathcote,' said the sergeant, as the remnant of a real English plum-pudding was put between him and his man by Mrs Growler.

'A little hotter than it is at home, eh?'

'Indeed it is. You must have had it hot last night, sir?'

'Very hot, sergeant. We had to work uncommonly hard to do it as well as we did.'

'It was not a nice Christmas game, sir, was it?'

'Eh, me!' said Mrs Medlicot. 'There's nae Christmas games or ony games here at all, except just worrying and harrying, like sae many dogs at each others' throats.'

'And you think nothing more can be done?' Harry asked.

'I don't think we shall catch the men. When they get out backwards it's very hard to trace them. He's got a horse of his own with him, and he'll be beyond reach of the police by this time to-morrow. Indeed, he's beyond their reach now. However, you'll have got rid of him.'

'But there are others as bad as he left behind. I wouldn't trust that fellow Boscobel a yard.'

'He won't stir, sir. He belongs to this country, and does not want to leave it. And when a thing has been tried like that and has failed, the fellows don't try it again. They are cowed like by their own failure. I don't think you need fear fire from the Boolabong side again this summer.'

After this the sergeant and his man discreetly allowed themselves to be put to bed in the back cottage; for, in truth, when they arrived, things had come to such a pass at Gangoil that the two additional visitors were hardly welcome. But hospitality in the bush can be stayed by no such considerations as that. Let their employments or enjoyments on hand be what they may, everything must yield to the entertainment of strangers. The two constables were in want of their Christmas dinner, and it was given to them with no grudging hand.

As to Nokes, we may say that he has never since appeared in the neighbourhood of Gangoil, and that none thereabouts ever knew what was his fate. Men, such as he, wander away from one colony into the next, passing from one station to another, or sleeping on the ground, till they become as desolate and savage as solitary animals. And at last they die in the bush, creeping, we may suppose, into hidden nooks as the beasts do when the hour of death comes on them.

CHAPTER XII

CONCLUSION

THE constables had started from Gangoil on their way to Boolabong a little after four, and from that time till he was made to get out of bed for his dinner Harry Heathcote was allowed to sleep. He had richly earned his rest by his work; and he lay motionless, without a sound, in the broad daylight, with his arm under his head—dreaming, no doubt, of some happy squatting land, in which there were no free-selectors, no fires, no rebellious servants, no floods, no droughts, no wild dogs to worry the lambs, no grass-seeds to get into the fleeces, and in which the price of wool stood steady at two shillings and sixpence a pound. His wife from time to time came into the room, shading the light from his eyes, protecting him from the flies, and administering in her soft way to what she thought might be his comforts. His sleep was of the kind which no light, nor even flies, can interrupt. Once or twice she stooped down and kissed his brow, but he was altogether unconscious of her caress.

During this time old Mrs Medlicot arrived; but her coming did not awake the sleeper, though it was by no means made in silence. The old woman sobbed and cried over her son, at the same time expressing her thankfulness that he should have turned up in the forest so exactly at the proper moment—evidently taking part in the conviction that her Giles had saved Gangoil and all its sheep. And then there were all the necessary arrangements to be made for the night, in accordance with which almost everybody had to give up his or her bed, and sleep somewhere else. But nothing disturbed Harry. For the present he was allowed to occupy his own room, and he enjoyed the privilege.

Kate Daly during this time was much disturbed in mind. The reader may remember—Kate at any rate remembered well—that just as the doctor had arrived to set his broken bone, Mr Medlicot, disabled as he was, had attempted to take her by the arm. He had certainly chosen an odd time for a declaration of love, just at the moment in which he ought to have been preparing himself for the manipulation of his fractured limb; but unless he had meant a declaration of love, surely he would not have seized her by the arm? It was a matter to her of great moment. Oh, of what vital importance! The English girl living in a town—or even in what we call the country—has no need to think of any special man till some special man thinks of her. Men are fairly plentiful, and if one man does not come another will. And there have probably been men coming and going in some sort since the girl left her schoolroom, and became a young lady. But in the bush the thing is very different. It may be that there is no young man available within fifty miles—no possible lover or future husband, unless Heaven should interfere almost with a miracle. To those to whom lovers are as plentiful as blackberries it may seem indelicate to surmise that the thought of such a want should ever enter a girl's head. I doubt whether the defined idea of any want had ever entered poor Kate's head. But now that the possible lover was there—not only possible but very probable—and so eligible in many respects, living so close, with a house over his head and a good business; and then so handsome and, as Kate thought, so complete a gentleman! Of course she turned it much in her mind. She was very happy with Harry Heathcote. There never was a brother-in-law so good! But, after all, what is a brother-in-law, though he be the very best? Kate had already begun to fancy that a house of her own and a husband of her own would be essential to her happiness. But then a man cannot be expected to make an offer with a broken collar-bone—certainly cannot do so just when the doctor has arrived to set the bone.

Later on in the day, when the doctor had gone and Medlicot was, according to instructions, sitting out on the verandah in an arm-chair, and his mother was with him, and while Harry was sleeping as though he never meant to be awake again, Kate managed to say a few words to her sister. It will be understood that the ladies' hands were by no means empty. The Christmas dinner was in course of preparation, and Sing-Sing, that villanous Chinese cook, had absconded. Mrs Growler, no doubt, did her best, but Mrs Growler was old and slow, and the house was full of guests. It was by no means an idle time, but still Kate found an opportunity to say a word to her sister in the kitchen.

'What do you think of him, Mary?'

To the married sister 'him' would naturally mean Harry Heathcote, of whom, as he lay asleep, the young wife thought that he was the very perfection of patriarchal pastoral manliness; but she knew enough of human nature to be aware that the 'him' of the moment to her sister was no longer her own husband.

'I think he has got his arm broken fighting for Harry, and that we are bound to do the best we can for him.'

'Oh, yes; that's of course. I'm sure Harry will feel that. He used, you know, to—to—that is, not just to like him, because he is a free-selector.'

'They'll drop all that now. Of course, they could not be expected to know each other at the first starting. I shouldn't wonder if they became regular friends.'

'That would be nice! After all, though you may be so happy at home, it is better to have something like a neighbour. Don't you think so?'

'It depends on who the neighbours are. I don't care much for the Brownbies.'

'They are quite different, Mary.'

'I like the Medlicots very much.'

'I consider he's quite a gentleman,' said Kate.

'Of course he's a gentleman. Look here, Kate. I shall be ready to welcome Mr Medlicot as a brother-in-law, if things should turn out that way.'

'I didn't mean that, Mary.'

'Did you not? Well, you can mean it if you please, as far as I am concerned. Has he said anything to you, dear?'

'No.'

'Not a word?'

'I don't know what you call a word. Not a word of that kind.'

'I thought perhaps—'

'I think he meant it once—this morning.'

'I dare say he meant it; and if he meant it this morning, he won't have forgotten his meaning to-morrow.'

'There's no reason why he should mean it, you know.'

'None in the least, Kate, is there?'

'Now you're laughing at me, Mary. I never used to laugh at you when Harry was coming. I was so glad, and I did everything I could.'

'Yes, you went away and left us in the Botanical Gardens. I remember. But, you see, there are no Botanical Gardens here, and the poor man couldn't walk about if there were.'

'I wonder what Harry would say if it were to be so?'

'Of course he'd be glad, for your sake.'

'But he does so despise free-selectors! And then he used to think that Mr Medlicot was quite as bad as the Brownbies. I wouldn't marry any one to be despised by you and Harry.'

'That's all gone by, my dear,' said the wife, feeling that she had to apologize for her husband's prejudices. 'Of course one has to find out what people are before one takes them to one's bosom. Mr Medlicot has acted in the most friendly way about these fires, and I'm sure Harry will never despise him any more.'

'He couldn't have done more for a real brother than have his arm broken.'

'But you must remember one thing, Kate. Mr Medlicot is very nice, and like a gentleman, and all that; but you never can be quite certain about any man till he speaks out plainly. Don't set your heart upon him till you are quite sure that he has set his upon you.'

'Oh, no!' said Kate, giving her maidenly assurance when it was so much too late.

Just at this moment Mrs Growler came into the kitchen, and Kate's promises and her sister's cautions were for the moment silenced.

'How we're to manage to get the dinner on the table I for one don't know at all,' said Mrs Growler. 'There's Mr Bates 'll be here; that will be six of 'em; and that Mr Medlicot will want somebody to do everything for him, because he's been and got hisself smashed. And there's the old lady has just come out from home, and is as particular as anything. And Mr Harry himself never thinks of things at all. One pair of hands, and them very old, can't do everything for everybody.' All of which was very well understood to mean nothing at all.

Household deficiencies—and, indeed, all deficiencies—are considerable or insignificant in accordance with the aspirations of those concerned. When a man has a regiment of servants in his dining-room, with beautifully cut glass, a forest of flowers, and an iceberg in the middle of his table if the weather be hot, his guests will think themselves ill-used and badly fed if aught in the banquet be astray. There must not be a rose-leaf ruffled; a failure in the attendance, a falling-off in a dish, or a fault in the wine, is a crime. But the same guests shall be merry as the evening is long with a leg of mutton and whisky toddy, and will change their own plates, and clear their own table, and think nothing wrong, if from the beginning such has been the intention of the giver of the feast. In spite of Mrs Growler's prognostications, though the cook had absconded, and the chief guest of the occasion could not cut up his own meat, that Christmas dinner at Gangoil was eaten with great satisfaction.

Harry had been so far triumphant. He had stopped the fire that was intended to ruin him, he had beaten off his enemies on their own ground, and he was no longer oppressed by that sense of desolation which had almost overpowered him.

'We'll give one toast, Mrs Medlicot,' he said, when Mrs Growler and Kate between them had taken away the relics of the plum-pudding. 'Our friends at home!'

The poor lady drank the toast with a sob. 'That's vera weel for you, Mr Heathcote. You're young, and will win your way hame, and see auld freends again, nae doubt; but I'll never see ane of them mair, except those I have here.' Nevertheless, the old lady ate her dinner, and drank her toddy, and made much of the occasion, going in and out to her son upon the verandah.

Soon after dinner, Heathcote, as was his wont, strayed out with his prime minister, Bates, to consult on the dangers which might be supposed still to threaten his kingdom, and Mrs Heathcote, with her youngest boy in her lap, sat talking to Mrs Medlicot in the parlour. Such was not her custom in weather such as this. Kate had been sent out on to the verandah, with special commands to attend to the wants of the sufferer, and Mrs Heathcote would have followed her had she not remembered her sister's appeal, 'I did everything I could for you.' In those happy days Kate had been very good, and certainly deserved requital for her services. And, therefore, when the men had gone out, Mrs Heathcote with her guest remained in the warm room, and went so far as to suggest that at that period of the day the room was preferable to the verandah. Poor Mrs Medlicot was new to the ways of the bush, and fell into the trap; and thus Kate Daly was left alone with her wounded hero.

When told to take him out his glass of wine, and when conscious that no one followed her, she felt herself to have been guilty of some great sin, and was almost tempted to escape. She had asked her sister for help; and this was the help that was forthcoming—help so palpable, so manifest, as to be almost indelicate! Would he think that plans were being made to catch him, now that he was a captive and impotent? The thought that it was possible that such an idea might occur to him was terrible to her. She would rather lose him altogether than feel the stain of such a suggestion on her own conscience. She put the glass of wine down on the little table by his side, and then attempted to withdraw.

'Stay a moment with me,' he said. 'Where are they all?'

'Mary and your mother are inside. Harry and Mr Bates have gone across to look at the horses.'

'I almost feel as though I could walk too.'

'You must not think of it yet, Mr Medlicot. It seems almost a wonder that you shouldn't have to be in bed, and you with your collar-bone broken only last night. I don't know how you can bear it as you do.'

'I shall be so glad I broke it, if one thing will come about.'

'What thing?' asked Kate, blushing.

'Kate—may I call you Kate?'

'I don't know,' she said.

'You know I love you—do you not? You must know it. Dearest Kate, can you love me and be my wife?'

His left arm was bound up, and was in a sling, but he put out his right hand to take hers—if she would give it to him. Kate Daly had never had a lover before, and felt the occasion to be trying. She had no doubt about the matter. If it were only proper for her to declare herself, she could swear with a safe conscience that she loved him better than all the world. 'Put your hand here, Kate,' he said. As the request was not exactly for the gift of her hand, she placed it in his. 'May I keep it now?' She could only whisper something which was quite inaudible, even to him. 'I shall keep it and think that you are all my own. Stoop down, Kate, and kiss me if you love me.'

She hesitated for a moment, trying to collect her thoughts. She did love him and was his own; still to stoop and kiss a man, who, if such a thing were to be allowed at all, ought certainly to kiss her! She did not think she could do that. But then she was bound to protect him, wounded and broken as he was, from his own imprudence; and if she did not stoop to him, he would rise to her. She was still in doubt, still standing with her hand in his, half bending over him, but yet half resisting as she bent, when, all suddenly, Harry Heathcote was on the verandah, followed by the two policemen, who had just returned from Boolabong. She was sure that Harry had seen her, and was by no means sure that she had been quick enough in escaping from her lover's hand to have been unnoticed by the policemen also. She fled away as though guilty, and could hardly recover herself sufficiently to assist Mrs Growler in producing the additional dinner which was required.

The two men were quickly sent to their rest, as has been told before; and Harry, who had in truth seen how close to his friend his sister-in-law had been standing, would, had it been possible, have restored the lovers to their old positions; but they were all now on the verandah, and it was impossible. Kate hung back, half in and half out of the sitting-room, and old Mrs Medlicot had seated herself close to her son. Harry was lying at full length on a rug, and his wife was sitting over him. Then Giles Medlicot, who was not quite contented with the present condition of affairs, made a little speech.

'Mrs Heathcote,' he said, 'I have asked your sister to marry me.'

'Dearie me, Giles!' said Mrs Medlicot.

Kate remained no longer half in and half out of the parlour, but retreated altogether and hid herself. Harry turned himself over on the rug, and looked up at his wife, claiming infinite credit in that he had foreseen that such a thing might happen.

'And what answer has she given you?' said Mrs Heathcote.

'She hasn't given me any answer yet. I wonder what you and Heathcote would say about it.'

'What Kate has to say is much more important,' replied the discreet sister.

'I should like it of all things,' said Harry, jumping up. 'It's always best to be open about these things. When you first came here I didn't like you. You took a bit of my river frontage—not that it does me any great harm—and then I was angry about that scoundrel Nokes.'

'I was wrong about Nokes,' said Medlicot, 'and have, therefore, had my collar-bone broken. As to the land, you'll forgive my having it if Kate will come and live there?'

'By George! I should think so. Kate, why don't you come out? Come along, my girl! Medlicot has spoken out openly, and you should answer him in the same fashion.'

So saying he dragged her forth, and I fear that, as far as she was concerned, something of the sweetness of her courtship was lost by the publicity with which she was forced to confess her love.

'Will you go, Kate, and make sugar down at the mill? I have often thought how bad it would be for Mary and me when you were taken away; but we shan't mind it so much if we know that you are to be near us.'

'Speak to him, Kate,' said Mrs Heathcote, with her arm round her sister's waist.

'I think she's minded to have him,' said Mrs Medlicot.

'Tell me, Kate—shall it be so?' pleaded the lover.

She came up to him, and leaned over him, and whispered one word which nobody else heard. But they all knew what the word was. And before they separated for the night, she was left alone with him, and he got the kiss for which he was asking when the policemen interrupted them.

'That's what I call a happy Christmas,' said Harry, as the party finally parted for the night.

EXPLANATORY NOTES

IN these notes the abbreviation *ATA* refers to the edition of the Australian section of Anthony Trollope's *Australia and New Zealand* (2 vols., 1873), edited by P. D. Edwards and R. B. Joyce and published by the University of Queensland Press in 1967 under the title *Anthony Trollope: Australia*.

3   *Christmas, 1871*: Anthony Trollope himself spent Christmas 1871 in Australia, but not at his son Frederic's sheep station, Mortray, which in many respects served as the model for Gangoil. His itinerary during his first visit to Australia in 1871–2 is summarized in Appendix 1 to *ATA*.

twenty-four years of age: the same age as Frederic James Anthony Trollope, the author's younger son, who was born on 27 September 1847. Other resemblances between Fred Trollope and Harry Heathcote are discussed in the Introduction to the present edition and in subsequent notes.

the younger three months: Fred Trollope did not marry until 14 December 1871, almost exactly the date on which the story of *Harry Heathcote of Gangoil* commences; but he and his wife Susannah (née Farrand) had two babies the same ages as those of Harry and Mary Heathcote by the time the novel was first published in England (Christmas 1873).

whole melted . . . nobbler . . . damper: after this initial barrage of Australianisms, Harry for the most part reverts to his mother tongue. A nobbler was a glass of spirits and damper was (and is) bread made from flour and water, without yeast. Trollope may also have intended Harry's adverbial use of 'whole', in the phrase 'whole melted', to sound characteristically Australian.

the end of February: like much else in the story old Bates's weather-lore, and the author's subsequent comment on the frequency of bushfires at Christmas, are applicable to more southerly latitudes—such as the centre-west of New South Wales, where Fred Trollope had his station—rather than to the subtropical Mary River valley, where Harry Heathcote has his. February is normally one of the wettest months of the year in south-east Queensland. There had been a major flood early in 1871, the year Anthony Trollope visited the district.

4   *a young squatter*: on 'squatters' and 'free-selectors' see Introduction to the present edition.

west of the Mary River in Queensland: this was not Trollope's initial choice of location. See above, Introduction. Fred Trollope's sheep station, Mortray, was in the centre-west of New South Wales, about 250 miles west of Sydney and 800 miles or more south of the imaginary Gangoil.

owned thirty thousand sheep of his own, was a magistrate in those parts: Fred Trollope had a smaller flock of a mere 10,000 sheep—not enough, as it turned out, to enable him to survive. His sheep station was sold during his father's second visit to Australia in 1875. He had been gazetted a magistrate in September 1872.

5   *got above him at school*: Fred Trollope, too, had emigrated to Australia partly because, as his father put it in his *Autobiography*, 'boys who did not grow so fast as he did got above him at school'.

120,000 acres: Mortray, Fred Trollope's station, was only a quarter the size.

6   *come to them from England*: 'I have been at many bush-houses . . . but at not one, as I think, in which I have not found a fair provision of books . . . The authors I found most popular were certainly Shakespeare, Dickens, and Macaulay . . . To have a Shakespeare is a point of honour with every man who owns a book at all,—whether he reads it or leaves it unread.' (*ATA* 313)

7   *interloper, like a free-selector*: see Introduction to the present edition.

9   *without an axe*: here Trollope is clearly drawing on memories of his trip by coach up the Mary River valley from Maryborough to Gympie. 'Woodland country in Australia . . . is called either bush or scrub. Woods which are open, and passable,—passable at any rate for men on horseback,—are

bush. When the undergrowth becomes thick and matted so as to be impregnable without an axe, it is scrub. In Queensland the scrubs are filled with tropical plants,—long vine tendrils, palms, and the parasite fig-tree . . .' (*ATA* 114).

10 *like troops of skeletons*: compare the almost proverbial lines in Dorothea Mackellar's poem 'My Country', 'The stark white ring-barked forests | All tragic to the moon'.

   would become insurmountable: 'But the wonder of the journey was in the badness of the roads and the goodness of the coachmanship . . . There is often no road, and the coach is taken at random through the forest.' (*ATA* 115).

11 *two ends of the house*: the description of the house is almost identical with that of Fred Trollope's at Mortray (*ATA* 307–8).

12 *on four wheels*: according to *OED*, four-wheel buggies were the American variety and two-wheel the English (or Indian). In fact both varieties were common in Australia.

14 *My word! little squall a coming*: Jacko's favourite exclamation, 'My word', used to be very common in Australian speech, but many of his other locutions, including 'a coming', sound more Cockney (perhaps Dickensian Cockney) than Australian.

16 *Duffer, indeed*: Harry uses the word 'duffer' in the sense that would be familiar to English readers, i.e. clumsy or inept person; but Jacko would have been more accustomed to its specifically Australian sense, i.e. cattle-stealer, and is perhaps pretending to take it that way.

20 *maintain thirty families*: the figure seems high, though a sugar farm with two hundred acres under cultivation was (and is) quite large. Most sugar-farmers depended on indentured labourers from the South Sea Islands, known as Kanakas, and these were all single men. See *ATA* chapter VIII and note to p. 37 below.

21 *said the German*: south-east Queensland was one of the main areas of German settlement in Australia. Trollope's choice of a German as one of Harry's sager counsellors is consonant

with the high regard in which German settlers were held in the colonies.

31 *Well, you go on*: possibly Trollope's rendition of the exclamation 'Go on', expressing surprise or disbelief, commonly used in Australia.

37 *had been ruined*: Trollope's son was 'ruined' less than two years later, but in his case ruin was precipitated by a three-year drought, not by bushfires.

South Sea Islands: see note to p. 20, above and *ATA* chapter VIII. The total cost of Island labour was less than 10*s.* a week, whereas white workers on the sugar plantations were paid about 25*s.* a week. There was widespread concern in England—not shared by Trollope—that the slave trade was being surreptitiously revived in Queensland half a century after it had been outlawed in all British possessions.

44 *off to Gympie*: gold had been discovered at Gympie, on the Mary River south of Maryborough, in 1867.

52 *certain old school-words*: perhaps from Longfellow's 'Excelsior'.

55 *Boolabong*: the name sounds like a fanciful compound of 'billabong' (backwater) and Bogalong and Goolagong, two townships quite close to Trollope's son's sheep station. All of the 'aboriginal' place-names in the novel (Gangoil, Boolabong, Coolaroo) appear to be imaginary. The editor of the *Graphic*, Arthur Locker, tried unsuccessfully to persuade Trollope to change the title of the novel, but whether or not because he disliked the name Gangoil is not clear (*The Letters of Anthony Trollope*, ii. 600): certainly Gangoil sounds neither euphonious nor convincingly 'aboriginal'.

for more than thirty years: the penal settlement at Moreton Bay, about 150 miles south of Gangoil, had been established in 1824. Most of the convicts were transferred to Sydney in 1839. Old Brownbie had presumably been freed ('emancipated') before then.

56 *before it was a colony*: Queensland had not become a separate colony until 1859. Trollope probably means before 1839, when the convict settlement at Moreton Bay was disbanded, or 1842, when Moreton Bay and the surrounding districts

(including the Mary River valley) were first officially thrown open to free-settlers.

57   *within 150 miles of Boolabong*: that is to say roughly as far south as Brisbane, the colonial capital.

58   *on the Sunday before it*: Trollope's manuscript and all previous printed texts read 'on the Monday before it'. But later references make it clear that the events described in this chapter in fact occurred on Sunday.

throughout the bush: 'The nomad tribe of pastoral labourers,—of men who profess to be shepherds, boundary-riders, sheep-washers, shearers, and the like,—form altogether one of the strangest institutions ever known in a land, and one which to my eyes is more degrading and more injurious even than that other institution of sheep-stealing . . . In the pastoral districts it is understood that when hospitality is demanded from a squatter it shall be given . . . The labouring man, with his "swag" over his back,—the "swag" being his luggage, comprising probably all the property he has in the world,—is sent to the "hut". There is a hut at every station, fitted up with bunks, in which the workmen sleep. Here the wanderer is allowed to stretch his blanket for the night,—and on all such occasions two meals are allowed to him. He has meat and flour in the morning, and meat and flour in the evening. Then he passes on his way.' (*ATA* 137–8)

59   *'shaken' the horse*: according to Eric Partridge (*A Dictionary of Historical Slang*) 'shake' in this sense was also current in England and America but had become mainly an Australianism by the end of the nineteenth century.

Darling Downs: the manuscript of the novel reads Darling Downs, but all previous printed texts have 'Darnley Downs'. There is no district in Queensland called Darnley Downs, and given that the district in question is obviously extensive—comprising a number of 'runs'—Trollope had no reason to invent a name for it. The Darling Downs are inland from Brisbane.

62   *'blowing'*: 'When one man asserts that he has shot a hundred and fifty wild horses in a day, it is natural that another man

should have shot two hundred. And so the thing grows . . .
The colonists themselves have a term for it, and call it—
"blowing".' (*ATA* 147) Trollope's advice to Australians, sol-
emnly iterated, and long held against him, was 'Don't blow!'
(*ATA* 148, 376) The expression, and presumably the practice, were also common in America in the late nineteenth
century.

66 *with her Bible in her hand*: Trollope's characters are not usually
so assiduous in their observance of the Sabbath, and he
notes in *ATA* (p. 315) that 'Sabbath-day observances are
laxly kept in the bush'. In this instance the explanation may
lie in the fact that *Harry Heathcote of Gangoil* is a Christmas
story.

67 *new chum*: 'The idea that Englishmen,—that is, new-chums,
or Englishmen just come from here,—are made of paste,
whereas the Australian, native or thoroughly acclimatized,
is steel all through, I found to be universal.' (*ATA* 413)

78 *of our spelling*: in his manuscript Trollope spelt the word
'puggerah'. He was not alone in his uncertainty about the
spelling. *OED* offers the choice of puggree or puggaree, to
which the *Collins Dictionary of the English Language* (1979) adds
pugree and pugaree. The Indian word later became the
standard term for the band worn around the slouch hat
issued to Australian soldiers.

79 *frontage to the water*: this rather detailed topographical description is surprising in view of Trollope's merely fleeting ac-
quaintance with the neighbourhood. It suggests that he may
have forgotten the main flow of the Mary River is from
south to north, not west to east.

81 *with their flocks*: Trollope is wrong. Captain Cook saw bushfires burning as he sailed up the east coast of Australia in
1770, eighteen years before the first European settlement.

84 *so well known in the bush*: the method of fighting bushfires that
Trollope has described is called backburning.

86 *loaded with leaves*: this was the most common mode.

92 *was capital in the colony of Queensland*: Harry's memory was
inaccurate. Under the Criminal Practice Act of 1865 the

only capital offences in Queensland were treason, piracy, murder, rape, and bushranging.

as Abraham no doubt exercised: in thinking of himself as an Abraham *manqué* Harry perhaps has hazy recollections of God's command to Abraham, 'Get thee out of thy country, and from thy father's house, unto a land that I will show thee: And I will make of thee a great nation', or God's promise, 'I will give unto thee, and to thy seed after thee, the land wherein thou art a stranger' (Genesis 12: 1–2, 17: 8). See also the Introduction to the present edition.

97   *the following day was Christmas*: in fact Christmas Day fell on a Monday, not a Tuesday, in 1871.

110 *John*: i.e. John Chinaman.

THE WORLD'S CLASSICS

A Select List

JANE AUSTEN: Emma
Edited by James Kinsley and David Lodge

WILLIAM BECKFORD: Vathek
Edited by Roger Lonsdale

JOHN BUNYAN: The Pilgrim's Progress
Edited by N. H. Keeble

THOMAS CARLYLE: The French Revolution
Edited by K. J. Fielding and David Sorensen

GEOFFREY CHAUCER: The Canterbury Tales
Translated by David Wright

CHARLES DICKENS: Christmas Books
Edited by Ruth Glancy

BENJAMIN DISRAELI: Coningsby
Edited by Sheila M. Smith

MARIA EDGEWORTH: Castle Rackrent
Edited by George Watson

SUSAN FERRIER: Marriage
Edited by Herbert Foltinek

ELIZABETH GASKELL: Cousin Phillis and Other Tales
Edited by Angus Easson

THOMAS HARDY: A Pair of Blue Eyes
Edited by Alan Manford

HOMER: The Iliad
Translated by Robert Fitzgerald
Introduction by G. S. Kirk

HENRIK IBSEN: An Enemy of the People, The Wild Duck,
Rosmersholm
Edited and Translated by James McFarlane

HENRY JAMES: The Ambassadors
Edited by Christopher Butler

A complete list of Oxford Paperbacks, including The World's Classics, OPUS, Past Masters, Oxford Authors, Oxford Shakespeare, and Oxford Paperback Reference, is available in the UK from the Arts and Reference Publicity Department (RS), Oxford University Press, Walton Street, Oxford OX2 6DP.

In the USA, complete lists are available from the Paperbacks Marketing Manager, Oxford University Press, 200 Madison Avenue, New York, NY 10016.

Oxford Paperbacks are available from all good bookshops. In case of difficulty, customers in the UK can order direct from Oxford University Press Bookshop, Freepost, 116 High Street, Oxford, OX1 4BR, enclosing full payment. Please add 10 per cent of published price for postage and packing.